the guy next door

Potter Lake Small Town Romance
Book Three

dl white

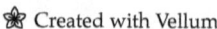

In memory of those that we have lost to cancer, in celebration of those who fought the fight.
For Ryan, who asked me every single day to put him in one of my books, so I did. Enjoy, my friend!

author's note

Whew, y'all. This book was a struggle.

It's been a long time (two years is a long time in writer years) since I published a full length novel, since I wrote something that made me proud to slap my name on it as the author.

This book is my victory lap. In the middle of writing it, I became very sick and put myself on hiatus. The first sign that I was feeling better was a renewed vigor to introduce the world to Taj and Evonne.

This book is inspired by my never-ending love for my favorite band (duh, *NSYNC) and watching the *New Edition* movie approximately 319 times. **The Guys Next Door** showed up in my brain, sat down, and wouldn't leave. Their former tenor, Taj, stepped out front to tell their story.

You will recognize Evonne from Curl & Dye and Second Time Around. If you haven't read them, I implore you to please read them and meet Evonne. She is fun and spunky, a lot like me, but also my exact opposite. I adore her, and I wanted her to have a happy ending.

I would love you to LOVE the story of Evonne and Taj, a spitfire itching to break out of a mold and an overly cautious cancer survivor who needs to live. If you do enjoy my books, please drop by any of your favorite retail sites and post up a positive review and talk it up!

Word of mouth sells books! Thanks, and Happy Reading!
DL White

the guy next door

one

. . .

EVONNE

Not that I was afraid because I was no punk, but the salon was scary at night.

Especially tonight, when storm clouds dampened the brightness of the moon, and the wind howled around the corners, pelting the plate glass windows with rain. The shadows had a way of playing tricks on me. A crash of thunder shook the strip mall that held The Curl & Dye, and I couldn't help it... I yelped.

I couldn't *wait* to get out of there.

I'd already rushed my last customer out, tying a spare scarf over her fresh hairdo and standing in the open doorway to make sure she got into her car. Then I pulled the double doors shut, flipped the OPEN sign to CLOSED, and locked myself in. A bolt of lightning ripped a seam in the inky dark sky. Seconds later, another sonic boom of thunder sent me running to the back room.

"If you had already moved out here, you wouldn't be too far from home right now."

I grabbed a few cleaning supplies from the closet and left them near the door, then started my evening ritual of poking a soft-bristled broom under each salon chair and gathering flyaway hairs that had escaped Leslie and Tamera's quick cleanup.

"Now you have to worry about driving back to Healy in this downpour."

I clicked my tongue, frustrated by my habit of procrastinating. I had more than enough saved to get a place in Potter Lake, a move I'd been putting off ever since I was hired full time at the salon. Two years ago, Potter Lake was a struggling town with nothing much to offer but a bunch of olden days shops and even older townspeople.

Then we got a new young mayor, and overnight, Potter Lake transformed into a mini-metropolis that prided itself on being a big little town. Mayor Cavanaugh was doing good things, establishing conveniences, and encouraging folks to set down roots and be a part of the community. New residents meant an increase in clientele, and between Leslie's salon and Kade's barbershop, there was no excuse to be walking around town with your hair looking like *'who did it and why'd they leave it that way'* as my Grandma Bobbie would phrase it.

Moving out to Potter Lake would make my life much more comfortable and far quieter, but I kept putting it off. Another month of inconvenience meant another few bucks in the bank. I could put up with my family for a month. Then the month would roll by, and I'd talk myself into another. Then another... and before I knew it, I was six months past my deadline and sick of screaming at my sister, Ebony, to pick up her half of our room.

"It's time just to do it," I declared, running a soft cotton towel over the appliances at my station. I was making good money at the shop, and sponsorship opportunities for my web channel, *Hair by E,* were starting to roll in.

And my parents finally seemed to not be angry anymore about that unfortunate incident that landed my ass back at home, ten years ago.

I wiped down every chair in the salon, using the orange scented leather cleaner that Leslie liked, cleaned out the shampoo bowl and refilled the pumps from the industrial sized storage containers. Leslie had already taken the day's deposit to the bank, so I tucked the evening's receipts in a locked drawer, checked my station for anything out of place, and pulled my jacket, which wasn't going to anything for me, off of its hook.

"I'm wearing this new wig, too. I'm about to be looking like a drowned rat."

I stepped outside and pulled the doors shut behind me, twisting the key into the lock as I went. I pulled the jacket up over my head, inhaled a sharp breath, and darted out into the pounding rain. The heel of my booties click-clacked against the uneven, pocked pavement as I made a mad dash for my car in the corner of the parking lot.

"And that's another thing…"

I sped into a jog as I neared my car. Key fob in hand, I fumbled with it to find the unlock button so I could get in.

"If you had yourself a man, you could have joined Leslie and Tamera for date night, but *Nah*. You have to be the hero and volunteer to work late so they can Netflix and chill. And what do you get out of it? Noth—"

The toe of one shoe caught a divot in the pavement, knocking me off balance. I flew forward, arms flailing before I thought to stick out at least one hand to break my fall. I hit the ground heavily and slid a few inches.

"Woo, *shit!*" I felt that in a major way, all the way up my arm.

I moaned in pain, pulling myself up on all fours, then tried to get my feet under me so I could stand. My jacket was no longer protecting my brand new wig, a sleek platinum blonde lace front, from the elements. Instead, it had landed in a pothole. Thankfully my bag ended up on top of it. I grabbed it by the handles and groped for the keys I had dropped.

And that's when I saw the blood.

I almost fainted, staring wide mouthed at the gash down the side of my palm to my wrist. Dark red rivulets mixed with rain and oozed down my arm, gathering at my elbow. Without thinking, I yanked the scarf from around my neck and wrapped it around my hand, then grabbed my keys, unlocked the car, and lurched for the driver's side door handle.

As soon as I fell into the car and dumped my bag on the passenger seat, I slammed the door against the torrents of rain. My arm was beginning to throb, the pain gaining a sharp edge to it. Blood seeped through the thin, emerald green silk scarf I'd worn to match my sweater.

Using my good hand, I dug through my purse to find my phone and dialed the first number that popped up— Tamera. "Shit!" I hissed when it went straight to voicemail. Same with Leslie. Then I remembered that Kade and Leslie, Erik and Tamera, and Kendrick and Monica were at the opening night festivities of the new Cineplex, one of those theaters where you could eat, drink and watch a movie. All of their phones would be off until the movie was over.

I selected the next number I could think of and prayed while it rang. Just when I thought it would roll over to voice-mail, the line picked up.

"Hullo?" A sleepy male voice answered.

"Romey!" I sat up, adding pep to my voice. "Hey, handsome. You in bed already?"

"Nah, I'm on the couch. Just tired. What you up to? You tryna come through? You need a teddy bear to comfort you through this storm, huh?"

I rolled my eyes but threw in a flirty giggle. "Mmm, maybe... I need a favor first."

"Unnh," he grunted, then made sounds like he was shifting positions. "I don't get paid 'til next week, so if you askin' for cash—"

"One time, I asked you for ten dollars, and now you act like I ask you for money all the time. Nobody wants your call center paycheck."

He grunted, sucking his teeth. "Vonne, what do you want? I'm tired."

"I'm stuck in Potter Lake. I fell in the parking lot and hurt myself; it's an open cut and bleeding bad—"

"So go to the hospital. What do you need me for?"

"Potter Lake doesn't have emergency services. They're gonna send me to Healy anyway. And I obviously can't drive to Healy if I'm bleeding to death."

"That is not an emergency, Drama Queen. You're way out there, and I just smoked. I can't get pulled over again. Plus, it's raining, and I got to save gas to get to work this week. But ay—"

He chuckled, then lowered his voice in an attempt to sound seductive. "If you get that situation worked out, you can roll by. I got somethin' you can sit on, make you feel better."

I exhaled so loudly he could probably hear it. "You are worthless to me, Rome. Count on me never sitting on anything belonging to you ever again."

"That's what we doin', Vonne? Don't call me for nothin' else."

"I don't call you for nothin' in the first place. You are strictly boredom relief. Bye, Rome."

I hung up before I could cuss him six ways to Sunday. Jerome, my infrequent dick appointment, was always grumpy when he was tired and high, but I might need him in the future, so it was best not to burn that bridge yet.

My next call was to Ebony, who was equally useless. "I'm working overnights this week," she said, probably as half-asleep as she sounded. She was an office manager for a transportation company, but she picked up extra hours dispatching. In my mind, I imagined her leaned forward, her forehead on her desk, snoring away before my call came through.

"Call 911. They'll come to get you."

"You got money for an ambulance transport bill?"

"I was trying to help," Ebony snapped. "Call Daddy. He'll fuss, but he'll come to get you."

I pondered this option but ultimately decided against it. My father was a warehouse foreman who worked an early shift. He needed his rest. Besides, help from my father would be accompanied by a free lecture from my mother about how I should have planned for things like this and not need them to bail me out every time I got into trouble.

"Nah, I'm not calling Daddy. I'll figure something out."

After making several calls that went unanswered, leaving a few voicemails and sending texts that seemed to fly into the ether and go nowhere, I dropped the phone in my lap. My wound was steadily staining the silk blouse I'd used to wrap my hand.

I felt lightheaded when I stared at it, so I closed my eyes and leaned forward onto the steering wheel.

two

. . .

TAJ

"You aren't having a heart attack, Mrs. Vaughn. It's only a gas bubble. You're going to be fine."

I grasped the age-spotted hands of Loretta Vaughn, a frequent patron of Lakeside Regional Clinic, and squeezed her. Ms. Loretta was a bona fide hypochondriac who came into the clinic at least twice a week, believing she had one severe ailment or another. Tonight, she thought she was having a heart attack because she had pain in her chest.

She had also, admittedly, overeaten at dinner and it could easily be gas. So, she'd come in to check.

After giving her the usual all-clear and a sample of Gas-X strips from the medical supply, I provided her with discharge papers, which were only health care tips— she felt better when I called them discharge papers, and guided her to the cushioned chairs in the waiting room.

I squatted in front of her, so I was level with her cloudy brown eyes. "Ms. Loretta, I can't release you to walk home in the rain." She lived in the housing complex right behind the clinic, and on a clear, warm evening, I would walk her home. "I called your nephew, and he's about done with his shift. He'll come by and pick you up in a while. That okay?"

Ms. Loretta nodded as always. This had been our routine since I started working at the clinic, and she felt safe enough to keep coming back. Satisfied, I stood.

"I bet I could find some sugar cookies and a cup of decaf coffee around here if I look hard."

Her face brightened, and she smiled, revealing lipstick on her teeth. "A few cookies would be nice. I don't like to have liquids too late. I'll be up and down all night, you know."

I stepped away before she could launch into a story I did not want to hear about the frequency of bathroom trips at her advanced age. I rounded the corner from the waiting room to the nurse's station. Jaslene, my partner for the evening, rolled her eyes as I walked past her. She customarily worked day shifts, but occasionally picked up extra hours.

"Her family needs to go ahead and put her at Primrose Gardens," she muttered. "She should not be living alone, wandering around town in the rain after dark."

"She doesn't live alone. She lives with her nephew."

Jas twisted in her chair, so her knees pointed toward me and folded her arms over her chest. "And where is *his* ass? Why are we babysitting Auntie while he's out doing God knows what—"

"*Officer* Vaughn patrols Potter Lake and the highway between here and Healy. He'll drop by when he makes his way back."

Silenced, Jaslene swiveled her chair back toward the desk, running her hand through her long ponytail as she did so. I rifled through the shelves on the other side of the check-in desk, then found it: an unopened package of sugar cookies that we kept around for the diabetes patients. I ripped them open, removed two from the package, set them on a napkin, and replaced the package on the shelf.

"She still shouldn't be by herself at night."

"What do you want him to do? Chain her to the radiator? You're just mad that you almost had to do some work."

"Whatever. I heard nights at the clinic were quiet. I don't need an old lady inventing diseases and messing with my easy hours."

I playfully tapped her shoulder as I passed her again, delivered the cookies to Mrs. Vaughn, and made sure she was warm and comfortable. She bit into a cookie, her eyes glued to the monitor mounted on the wall. She liked the Home TV channel, so when she was the only person in the clinic, I indulged her. I turned up the volume and slid the remote into the empty seat next to her.

Back at the desk, I settled into my seat to finish updating Mrs. Vaughn's patient record. If she happened to come back when I wasn't on shift, which never happened because most of the staff treated her like a crazy old lady, the nurse would see my notes from this evening's treatment: Gas X and sugar cookies.

I closed down the notes program and minimized the application, revealing the computer desktop with the clinic logo across the screen. Lakeside Regional was a brand new clinic, built out of a need for a larger health care facility. Dr. Elias Moore, Potter Lake's oldest and most prominent physician, had been operating with a few partners out of an older building that hadn't met code in over a decade.

A grant from the Mayor's foundation and assistance from the state provided money to build a facility for non-emergency services and office space for Potter Lake's physicians. Life-threatening incidents were still routed to Healy General, but for the occasional scrape, regular visits, or the town hypochondriac visit, the clinic filled the hole just fine.

"This is perfect writing weather," I mused, my chin in my palm while I watched the rain splatter the windows. "I could be at the piano, listening to the storm sounds and working out some tunes."

"Mmmmm," Jaslene hummed, a perfectly arched eyebrow tipping up like I knew it would. "Or working out some*one*."

I ignored her comment and reached under the desk for my bag. We had hooked up a few times and might hook up a few times more, but I wasn't in the mood for sex-tinged banter. Besides, what made messing with Jaslene fun was sneaking around.

My nylon bag whispered softly as I pulled it from its usual hiding spot. I unearthed a spiral-bound notebook and flipped it open to the page I'd been working on earlier, its place held by my favorite pen. In my spare time, I liked to journal, write down my thoughts and feelings. Most of the time, they were just words. Other times, they turned into more.

One could say I worked in the music business, in the most behind-the-scenes, on-the-fringes way possible. I'd been lucky enough to write songs that landed on albums and made life comfortable. Unless someone were paying close attention to the outer edges of the industry more than a decade ago, they'd never recognize my face, never know how close Taj Wright came to unimaginable fame and success.

A pair of headlights flashed past the double doors. A small coupe swerved into the lot, parked diagonally across several spaces, and screeched to a stop. Mrs. Vaughn's nephew drove a black Cadillac, so that wouldn't be him.

"Incoming," I called to Jaslene, who had left the desk and gone into the office equipment room.

"I'm busy," was her immediate response.

"Aww... did I hurt your little feelings?"

"You know what, Taj? You can fu—"

"Help! Help me, please!"

A woman stumbled through the sliding doors; one hand was wrapped in an emerald green scarf. Her hair was plastered to her head, a shock of blonde that I imagined was a nice contrast against her deep brown skin tone when it didn't resemble a dead animal.

I waved her in since she could obviously walk but was standing just inside the door, dripping onto the mat. She rushed forward, dumping a bag on the counter in front of her.

"I slipped and fell, and I managed to slice my hand clean open and it's bleeding but I live in Healy and I wasn't sure if I should drive all that way if it's this bad—"

"Okay, okay," I interrupted, pulling up the patient application and opening a new record. "First things first. Name."

"Evonne," she chirped, spelling it out for me. "E-v-o-n-n-e . Last name Girard. This hurts like a bitch, and I think I've lost a lot of blood."

I glanced up at her arm and the dried trail from the wrist to the elbow. Then I saw the scarf, assessing that it wasn't soaked. She had probably stopped bleeding.

"You haven't lost that much blood, Miss... Girard," I finished after checking the screen. "Insurance?"

"Uhm, yeah." She dug through the bag and produced a wallet. "I was hoping you could patch me up so I could at least drive home without dripping blood everywhere."

"Sure. But first I have to get you into the system. Do you have an insurance card?"

"Can we do this *after* you stop me from bleeding to death?"

I pulled my fingers back from the keyboard, ready to give back all the attitude I was getting. But I stopped when I saw wild panic glowing in almond-shaped brown eyes and throughout the delicate features of her face. Her brows were knit together, deep wrinkles of concern across her forehead, and she was so visibly stressed, she was nearly hyperventilating.

I rolled my chair back and grabbed a clipboard already prepped with paperwork. "Leave your insurance card at the front desk and follow me. Jas?"

A grunt from the back room said she knew that I wanted her to continue processing our emotional patient into the system while I took care of the wound. I led her to an exam room, gesturing to her to hop up onto the bed—the sanitary paper crinkled under her body.

"I'm going to get some tools so I can check that out and get you stitched up."

"Thank you, doctor." She sounded relieved.

I stuck my head back around the corner. "Actually," I said, flipping my badge at her. "Taj Wright, Registered Nurse. And if you have anything slick to say about a male nurse, I will let you bleed to death. We straight?"

three

. . .

TAJ

"*Owww!*"

My patient flinched, howling in my ear. I'd been pulling bits of gravel and dirt from the open wound down the side of her palm with a pair of surgical tweezers. It wasn't as bad as I'd thought it would be, but she had picked up some debris, and I needed to clean the wound so I could close it.

"Miss Girard," I said calmly, tightening my grip on her hand. "I need you to hold still."

"Okay, Nurse Dude..." She snatched her hand back, cradling it in the other. Her eyes were full of fire as she fumed. "That shit hurts!"

"There's no way to do this that doesn't hurt. If you want it to be clean, so it's not infected and correctly sutured, this is the way it's done."

"Can't you put me under, like at the dentist? Do you have any morphine? Or some Oxy...whatever?"

I masked my laughter with a cough. "We don't administer opiates or narcotics for this, Miss Girard."

"Stop calling me *Miss* Girard like you're trying not to say *bitch*. My name is Evonne."

"Okay, *Evonne*. My name is Taj, not *Nurse Dude*."

When she didn't respond, I hiked an eyebrow and held out my hand. She laid hers in my palm. Her leg began to twitch, and her eyes focused on everything but my careful cleaning of her wound.

"I need to swab with an antiseptic, and that's going to sting."

"Okay," she muttered. After a moment, she added, "Thanks for the warning."

I moved quickly, minimizing the pain by not drawing it out. When the wound was clean, I gave two quick pumps of an antibacterial spray and opened a package of butterfly sutures.

"I'm going to pull the wound closed and apply a few of these to hold it, then bandage it up. It should start to heal pretty quickly."

"Wait, you don't have to sew it up? That's what I was bracing for."

"Nope." I talked while I worked, gently applying the sutures. "It's not deep enough for that. I'll cover it with gauze and give you a few extra pads. Change it daily or as needed. Give it some air in a couple of days; that'll encourage healing. You should be back in business in no time. How did you do this again?"

"I work over at the Curl & Dye, on the other side of the lake." She paused, lifting her gaze to mine, looking for an indication that I'd heard of the place. I hadn't lived in Potter Lake long, but I had heard the story of the dueling salons. And how the owners were married now. "Anyway, I was trying to get to my car, and I tripped."

She paused to inspect the bandage I had applied and taped into place. "Should I be able to work with this? Considering I use my hands."

I shrugged, swiveling my stool away from her. "Sure. No tendons were cut; there was no muscle damage. You should regain mobility with some physical therapy—"

"Really, Nurse Dude?" Her very pretty, thick lips pursed. "You're giving me shit? I could have bled to death."

I laughed openly this time, beginning to clean up the tray I had been using. I rolled my stool back and laughed again. "You could not have bled to death from that superficial wound. So yes, I very much am giving you shit."

"I could get an infection and develop Gangrene, and then my hand could fall off. I heard on this *Doctor Danger* podcast—"

"Your limbs will not fall off, Miss Girard. I promise."

Her eyes narrowed. She was irritated, but this was the most fun I'd had all night. "Do you treat all your patients like this?"

"Just the overdramatic ones." I picked up the tray with discarded wrappers and unused sutures. "Don't get your bandage wet, but you should heal right up in a couple of days, a week tops, Miss Girard. I mean, Evonne."

"Thank you, Nurse Dude. I mean, Taj."

I led her back to the front desk and slid the visit paperwork across the counter. She signed the forms where initialed, and I handed her the carbon copy. I noticed her address said Healy, Georgia.

"You're driving into town tonight? In that weather?" She nodded, pressing her lips together. Suddenly, she seemed exhausted. "Be careful out there. Do you want a cup of coffee before you leave?"

She stuffed the papers into her bag and slipped it over her shoulder. "I want to be tired enough to fall right into bed when I get home. Thanks, Nurse Taj."

I waved as she walked out, and the doors slid closed behind her.

"Might wanna pick your tongue up off the floor."

Jaslene. I'd forgotten she was even in the room.

"You're driving to town? Ooh, be careful! Want some coffee?" She mocked me with a hand on one hip, repeating my words back to me. "Why didn't you just fuck her in the exam room?"

I rolled my head toward her, glared and rolled it back to the computer screen. "Because I'm a professional. Jealousy is ugly on you, Jaslene. Did Mrs. Vaughn go home?"

"Yeah." She sat in her chair and scooted to the other end of the desk. "Her nephew finally showed up to take that crazy old lady home. And ain't nobody *jealous*. Been there, ran through that," she reminded me, directing her eyes from my head to my feet and back up.

"Mmmmm. That's why you have an attitude right now."

She swung her hair behind a shoulder and got up again, marching to the back room. I picked up my abandoned notebook, my eyes falling on lyrics that I'd been working on for most of the week. The theme was elusive; I needed to do more than croon about a woman's curves.

The mood that I'd been trying to tap into before I was interrupted rolled back in. Cold, dark, somber vibes brought tones of a slow, sensual melody.

I scratched a few words across the page, humming lightly, newly inspired by visions of my latest patient lurking in the back of my mind.

four

. . .

EVONNE

That wicked weather from a few nights ago had blown right through and now moist, sticky heat beamed through my windshield at 9 AM.

The drive home to Healy that night had sealed the deal for me. I had to find a place to live in Potter Lake, sooner rather than later and before I could put it off again. I scoured the newspaper ads and found a few places I wanted to tour. I'd made an appointment to view one of them before my first client at the salon.

I pulled into the wide driveway of a large home and parked behind a car already sitting there. The driver's side door opened, and the realtor I was meeting stepped out, flashing me one of those fake salespeople smiles.

"Miss Girard?" The realtor called, approaching with her hand out.

Since I was still bandaged and tender, I waved awkwardly. "Evonne, please. You must be Kate."

"I am. I know you only have a little bit of time, so let's begin outside, shall we?"

She began her rehearsed spiel about the property. The owner had recently completed renovations. He lived in the house and would be my landlord. The addition that I was touring was more of a small guest house and had a private entrance, but I could also get into the house through the garage. The lease included an assigned parking spot and full use of the yard, including a pool and a deck with a barbecue grill. I liked that the home appeared new and well cared-for and that the owner would be near. I was no "Miss Fix It," and my dad would be twenty miles away.

"The home has one bedroom, one bath; however, it's roomy and very bright. The owner had the floors retiled, new carpet installed, new paint, the whole nine yards."

Kate babbled, pointing at things while she talked. "There's a nice sized kitchen, new appliances including a dishwasher, washer, and dryer." She waved a hand across the living and dining rooms, blowing past a sliding glass door leading to a brick patio and the backyard. "Let's take a look at the bedroom, hmmm?"

By the time I had toured the bedroom, bathroom, closet, investigated the garage and the storage shed behind the house, I was in love. It wasn't much, but I didn't need much after squeezing into a basement bedroom with Ebony for the last ten years.

The best part was that it wasn't far from the Curl & Dye, only a ten-minute drive over the bridge.

"The owner works quite a bit, some strange hours. You may not see him often. I think he's a doctor or something? That's why he's using a realty company to show the house."

She scrunched her nose with a *you understand* expression. "He said to assure any potential tenants that he is always a phone call away. The lease is for six months and is inclusive of utilities, including wireless internet. You'd have to arrange basic cable, satellite, or anything else."

She paused, seeming to inhale a long, fortifying breath. "Any questions?"

I glanced around at... *everything*. The house was steps away from a sprawling home with floor to ceiling windows and a lush yard. The neighborhood was all new builds. Sleek luxury cars sat in the driveways all down the street.

"What's the catch?" I asked, putting it plainly. "Is the place haunted? Did someone die here? Is the landlord an asshole? It seems too good to be true. Too... perfect."

They talked about neighborhoods like this one all the time on The Butler Did It.

Kate shrugged, pulling the straps of her bag onto her shoulder. "It's Potter Lake. It's too far for Healy kids, and the younger crowd wants to be in the new apartment complex downtown. It's a tiny space, already furnished, close to a larger home. Not ideal for a lot of people. The owner is seeking a particular kind of tenant."

I nodded, understanding perfectly. This was high salary, big house, two-car garage, fluffy white dog, and two-point-five-kids territory, not a hip, happening spot for a young single.

By age twenty, life had been *happening* so hard that I was asked to remove myself from the grounds of Spelman College. I was all done with the hip scene. I would take suburban life in a heartbeat.

"I'll bite," I told Kate, walking with her toward our cars. "I have plenty saved so I could make the deposit and first month's rent, no problem. I work near here, so this would be a nice place for me to jump to."

"Great." She flashed that fake smile again and reached into her bag for her keys. "I'll email you the application, and we'll get started. He does have a few applicants already, so get it back to me today if you'd like to be considered."

My heart skipped a beat. It was on.

five

. . .

TAJ

My realtor's annoyance was evident through her short, pointed sentences.

"This is the final applicant. I took the liberty of pre-checking her background and history. Except for an incident ten years ago, she's clean. She has family nearby and has held a steady job for the past 36 months. She's about the best you're going to get and would be a perfect tenant. You should heavily consider her application.

I opened the attachment, unbothered by her rude-adjacent email. Applicants took the process more seriously when professionals handled it. I'd been searching for the perfect tenant for months but wasn't impressed by the applicants Kate had brought to me. If someone was going to be living a stone's throw from my personal living space with access to my home, I wanted to have a good feeling.

I was stalling, and Kate was getting sharp about it. I opened the attachment and smiled when I saw the name on the top line: *Evonne Girard.*

As in, the owner of those smoky brown eyes and those

thick lips that had been haunting my memories. I laughed aloud, rubbing my palms together.

"Surprise move from your chess-by-mail partner?"

Jaslene tossed a couple of thick patient files in my direction and leaned against the desk, a hand on a shapely hip. We hadn't worked together since that stormy night, and her attitude seemed to have recovered from being rejected. Enough to flirt again, at least.

"Nah. just…I think I finally found a tenant."

"Oh." Her pink-tinted lips poked out in a pout. "You're not gonna let me live in your extra house, then?"

I'd thought it was one of those post coital utterings, something a person said in the heat of a moment but didn't mean. We'd had a great meal, a few glasses of potent wine, and more than a few rounds of pretty decent sex. She blurted out that she wouldn't mind living in the guest house so that I had access to her whenever I wanted her.

I laughed it off, not at all considering letting a woman I was playing with live in my house. Besides, she made most of the moves in our situationship and she'd rarely been denied. I already had access to her whenever I wanted her.

I studied her, then looked away, then gave her my full attention. "Jas, I didn't think you were serious about that. Were you?"

She snorted a laugh and hopped right up, feigning busyness with the stacks of folders on the desk. "No, I'm not serious! Can you even imagine us living that close to each other? We'd never get out of bed."

She snorted again, then conveniently found something to do in the back room.

I replied to the open email, telling Kate that the applicant was approved, though I hadn't read anything past her name. As long as she passed the background check and could have the required funds available, she was welcome to the place.

The ringer on my phone had been turned down so low I

barely heard it, but I felt it tucked away in the breast pocket of my scrubs. I pulled it up before it could roll to voicemail.

"What up, Bro-ski?" I practically yelled.

"Nothin' much Bro-tastic."

Cash Bridgeman was always nonchalant, slow to speak, with a southern drawl that no one else in his family seemed to have. "Going through some boxes in my parent's basement, getting them ready for their move. I found our demo tape, and I was listening to it."

In that instant, a wave of nostalgia hit.

The Guys Next Door was an R&B group I had been a part of since I was a kid. We started as any typical boy group started. We were friends, went to school together, lived in the same neighborhood. We'd sit around and sing along to the radio. Offhand, one of our moms mentioned that we sounded good together. We went back to singing but paid attention to the way we sounded together.

We played at it mostly, singing at church and in talent shows. As we grew older and our voices blended into a more mature and soulful sound, we booked openings for groups coming through town. We worked as much as we could, which wasn't much because our moms were adamant that we stayed in school and kept our grades up. We still had chores at home, participated in school activities whenever possible, but we also would take a trip to sing at the drop of a hat.

Davon James, Marquise Hillman, Corey Bridgeman, and I each had a job. Davon and I worked the music; Quise was good at coming up with steps and figuring out our stage blocking— who went where at what part of the song. Corey, who we called Cash, was our point person for booking and payment. His dad was an accountant, so he helped us manage what little money we made.

We never thought much would come of our group. We were the most professional amateurs we could be and singing was something fun to do, but none of us had any connections that would push us out further.

Until we opened for an up and coming R&B group called Tender Love Connection and unbeknownst to us, some heavy hitters were in the crowd. All hell broke loose.

By the end of the week, we'd signed a management deal and were invited to record a demo tape. Though we were based in Jacksonville, Florida, we started booking gigs across the south. Since it was summer, my mother, who was a teacher, could join us, giving us the freedom to take advantage of the spotlight shining on us.

We were on the cusp of something great. We could *feel* it. Every night was filled with excited whispers about all that had happened that day and what was happening the next.

When I started losing weight, I didn't think much of it. We were working hard, rehearsing every day, and the excitement produced nonstop adrenaline. Then came unexplainable bouts of severe fatigue, swollen glands, stomach pains. Mom insisted I take some time off.

"You're doing too much, Taj," she said, fussing while packing my bag. "You need a weekend at home with no excitement. Simmer down, get your bearings."

I wasn't feeling better in a few days, so she dragged me to our family doctor. That appointment sent up red flags, and by the end of the day, I was headed to oncology.

Non-Hodgkin Lymphoma wasn't a death sentence, my mother had been told. But it was serious enough that there was no way I was going on tour with the group.

I had been quickly replaced by a new artist named Terrell. He had a similar voice to mine, but he was older. Our manager thought he would loop in the demographic in his age group and mature the sound of Guys Next Door. No one knew him, but the label said the guys were lucky that he was available and willing to fill in. It was supposed to be temporary until I was better.

Later that year, I watched, from a chemo drip, as my friends, my brothers, what was once my future hit the stage at the BET Awards. They shot into the stratosphere from there.

And I hadn't sung with The Guys Next Door in fifteen years.

"The folks are finally making the big move?" I asked Cash.

We had all lived within blocks of each other, growing up. My family would be the last ones still in the neighborhood. Marquise moved his brothers across town to live with their grandmother. Davon retired his parents and moved them to Ft. Lauderdale.

"Yeah, they held out as long as they could, but they want something new and to be closer to the water. Not to mention, the grandkids keep coming." Cash had two sisters, both of whom had children. He had two of his own.

"I guess that makes sense. So, you found some stuff you can use to blackmail us, hold over our heads or something?"

Cash laughed. "A couple snaps of some big head kids out at the beach and stuff. I'm keeping those for our Lifetime Achievement Award Ceremony. I was mostly watching tapes of the early stuff, like our first performance. You remember?"

I'd started laughing before he even finished his sentence. We were off-key and bumping into each other through the whole first song. We got it together, eventually, but the video evidence will show that by the time we signed our deal, The Guys Next Door had come a mighty long way.

"Hey, remember this one?" Cash hummed the melody to *She's So Sweet*, a mid-tempo dance tune that was very familiar to me since I wrote it with Dav. The girls loved it since it was complimentary. Parents loved that it was only slightly suggestive.

"Remember it?" I cackled. "I dreamt that song for a year and a half, after singing it all summer."

"And *We Rock This Party*? That was a fan favorite."

"Yeah, yeah. That one, too."

I grinned, thinking of the futuristic trip-hop beat that Dav had put on the song. It sped up the flow and made it peppy and fun to dance to. We were well ahead of our time, music-wise. We'd listened to so many songs, so many bands, analyzed the Top 40 to try to determine the secret sauce. What made a song a hit? What tanked a group? And what could we do to avoid it?

"What are you doing with yourself these days, besides moving the folks?"

"A whole lot of nothing," he answered. "We went on hiatus after our last album. The break wasn't supposed to be this long. Not three years, you know?"

He paused, his long exhale crackling over the line. "We've had some personnel issues."

"Finally kicking Terrell out?"

"All over but the paperwork. But first, we had to get Quise through rehab. His grandma dying put a hurt on him."

I nodded, my mood solemn. Each of the guys had been through their hell. Marquise lost his parents in a car accident. His grandmother had raised his brothers and when she died of cancer, it was a low blow to him. He turned to liquor and pills to heal his pain, and after he'd totaled a brand new Escalade, he got off easy by paying a hefty fine and completing court-ordered rehab.

Cash was in a constant tug of war between the mothers of his children, back and forth to court with requests to get some benefit the other wasn't getting. Davon never liked to sit still. He'd attempted a jump to solo, but his album was dead on arrival and a severe hit to his ego.

And Terrell...

Well, Terrell had always and only been about himself and his career. He was doing fine, better than any of the other members. And that was the problem. He'd stepped outside of the group early in the game and took every opportunity to be out front and draw attention to himself. Things had finally come to a head and the group decided, at the end of their label contract, to take a hiatus before signing another deal.

"We've been talking lately," said Cash, "about going back to some of the old stuff and updating it. Bringing the fans into the process, you know? Let them vote on their classic favorites, then bring those back. Maybe writing some new stuff, but also getting back to our roots, being about the music and not about trying to hit Billboard."

He paused, pushing out a little huff and clicking his tongue. "We don't want to relaunch The Guys Next Door without the original crew. We need you, man."

His words shot a pang through my chest. "What do you need me for? You have Terrell."

"Naw, we ain't got Terrell. We never *had* Terrell. Terrell had *us*. We were stepping stones to his stardom. Terrell ain't Taj. He don't do nothin' but work out and oil up his six pack. He doesn't write, he doesn't play an instrument, he doesn't choreograph, he sucks at math—"

"But he's got a good voice," I interrupted. "The rest of you fill in around him. That's all you need. Not every group has to be best friends—"

"He's always sounded off; I know you hear it. He doesn't have the sound, the vision, or the history we all have. There's no nostalgia for him. He thinks our old stuff is corny and he won't sing it. He and Davon aren't speaking because Terrell had some words about *We Rock This Party*. He said it was juvenile and simplistic. It's not a perfect jam, but you know how hard he worked on that song."

"Man, yeah. Don't insult an artist's work to his face." Dav was sensitive about his shit when we were kids. He was probably even worse now.

"Mr. Good Voice has been doing solo work. No one has heard from him in months. We couldn't meet up if we wanted to— he don't return phone calls or email. That's not fair to the rest of us, you know? We're not accessories. We're not Terrell

Hawkins and The Guys Next Door. He ain't no Diana Ross, and we ain't the fuckin' Supremes."

I laughed. "Not Lionel Richie and The Commodores. I bet Terrell pulls more cash than everybody."

"You know my dad's been all over that for a minute. Even if I hadn't seen his contract, I've seen his house and his cars. He ran out of shit to buy, he makes so much money. His cut of our royalties is ridiculous, with his features on top of that. And he lives wild, you know what I'm saying? I'm not saying we're angels ourselves, but that blowback is going to hit us, and we're not getting paid enough to cover him."

Cash paused, but the silence was full. I understood what he was saying and how he was feeling about it. And if Cash, the most laid back member, was upset, I could only imagine how the other guys felt.

"If we ever sing again as a group," he continued, "it'll be without Terrell Hawkins. None of us want him back. We want TDub. So, you comin' back bro? Is you a Guy Next Door or nah?"

I lowered my head, resting my chin in my palm.

My writing credits on our songs meant that I made good money, though I wasn't recording, performing or touring. Adding the stage show back into my life would bring every-thing full circle, put me right back where I wanted to be when I was fourteen.

But my mind always boomeranged back to the life I'd built. My BSN didn't come easily. Fighting cancer had put me behind in school. I wasn't sure I'd make it, but I passed the NCLEX, the licensing exam for nursing, and worked at a hospital in Jacksonville while I wrote songs, some for The Guys Next Door.

I took a leap of faith and applied for an RN position at Lakeside Regional before it even opened. A prime position at a brand new facility in a small town, a nice mix of older and younger patients, plus the slower pace and hometown atmosphere was the breath of fresh air that I needed.

And it got me out of Jacksonville, where my dream died.

I'd worked hard to get to where I was. I was going to leave stability and a normal life behind for... *what*? To hop on stage in some ridiculous but fashionable leather getup, pump my hips and sing in four-part harmony about what I wanted to do to a woman?

I shrugged, though Cash couldn't see me. "I don't know, man. I live in Georgia; I bought a house. I have a job. It'd be tough to—"

"The only reason you left the group was because you were sick. You would still be with us if it weren't for that, right? You've been in remission for how long now?"

Cash knew the answer and would still make his point even if I didn't tell him. "A while," I answered quietly. My most recent scan, a year ago, had come back cancer-free. The chances of recurrence grow smaller when a patient has been in remission for five years. I was twice beyond that.

"But that doesn't—"

"So, it's safe to say you're good. You've *been* in the clear. I know you're scared to say it, but you're good, man. You're livin' safe and scared, but you can't run from this TDub," he said earnestly. "It's in you."

I blew out a breath, slouching enough that my head could rest on the back of the chair. "I don't know if I can go backward. And I don't know if I want to."

Cash exhaled a heavy breath. I knew he felt like he could talk me into it. I regretted that he couldn't, but I'd put too much work into recovery, not only my body but my mind and my spirit. Becoming a nurse was about way more than a regular paycheck, and building a real person's career for myself; I was on a mission.

I needed to give back what was given to me, so the

boyhood dream of being a pop superstar was going to have to stay in my dreams.

six

. . .

EVONNE

Ebony blew into our bedroom like a tornado, as was her habit.

Her bag went in one direction, her jacket in another. She plopped down at the end of my bed and reached toward her feet to unzip and pull off her boots, then threw them one by one, in the general area of the closet. She then flopped onto her back and rolled over to face me.

I sat cross-legged, laptop and notepad in front of me, earbuds in my ears.

"Did you listen to the new episode of The Butler Did It? Wasn't that wild?"

"Listening to it now," I told her, pressing pause on my phone app and pulling out an earbud. She and I were fans of podcasts, especially beauty and murder shows, and kept each other updated on all of our favorites. "Don't spoil it. Are you going to leave your shoes in the middle of the room? I cleaned up, in case you didn't notice."

She paused, glancing around our messy-unless-I-cleaned-it living space with heavily made-up eyes and overextended faux lashes. She went all out when she dressed for work, in form fitting tees, skintight jeans, and stiletto boots to sit at a computer all day. Her office mates were usually younger men that came in to drop off paperwork, pick up a check or a new assignment. Ebony ran the front office, and since they did a lot of work for AAA, the days could get busy, with lots of traffic in and out. She believed in playing the odds and figured one of them, at some point, would notice her and whisk her away.

"Oh," she replied, with a casual glance around the room and the shrug of one shoulder. "Yeah, I'll put my boots away in a minute. Hey Vonnie, can you order me a wig? I want something long and red."

"I keep telling you," I muttered, chewing on my thumbnail, scrolling one of my sponsor's websites. "You don't have the skin tone for the red hair you want. You'd look like Shenaenae from Martin. Or a brown Ronald McDonald."

"What about auburn? Or highlights, something subtle—"

"Evonne! Ebony!" My mother's bellow sounded from the top of the stairs. "There's laundry to fold. The boys have uniforms that need to be ironed. And dinner is about ready to set the table. Always hiding downstairs when there's work to be done!"

I sighed, quietly because Rhonda Girard could hear a sigh from a mile away. Fearless Ebony sucked her teeth and pushed off of the bed, then stomped toward the stairs. Ebony could get away with mumbling; I could not.

"Emmett and Edwin got to learn how to iron without burning a hole in stuff. I swear they do that on purpose, so they don't have to do it themselves."

Ten years ago, I showed up on the doorstep of my childhood home after being asked to leave Spelman, my mother's alma mater.

I was *still* paying penance for being found drunk,

sprawled on the lawn of a prestigious institution of learning, for wasting their money and shaming them so deeply that they could hardly show their faces at church.

I trudged up the stairs into the large, sunny kitchen. Mama had baked chicken and prepared some sides, so I set everything out on the table, while Ebony set plates, silverware, glasses, and napkins at each spot. The family gathered around the table, including Grandma Bobbie. She made every meal lively with talk of the town.

I listened and ate, monitoring my little brothers who were eight years apart but acted like toddlers when they were together. They would start a food fight at the drop of a hat.

My cell phone buzzed in the pocket of the leggings I had changed into when I got home from the salon. There was a strict 'no electronics at the table' rule, but I pulled it up and snuck a peek at the screen. My heart leaped into my throat.

It was an email from the realtor. The subject line read *Congratulations!*

———

The night the countersigned lease came through, I couldn't contain my excitement. I was sure my parents would be so proud of me, so I bounded into their bedroom, hardly able to speak.

Mama wore her blue polyester house dress comfortably wedged into her faded plaid lounger with a pile of sewing in her lap. The boys went through socks like crazy, but instead of buying new ones, she insisted on patching up the holes and putting those socks back into their drawers.

My father was laid out on the bed in threadbare lounge pants, a t-shirt, and black ankle socks, lightly snoring with one eye open. The TV, nearly as old as I was, in its wood cabinet and blurry tube display, blared NCSI as per their nightly ritual. They watched all the renditions-the regular series, the LA series and even the New Orleans series. If NCSI was on TV, they were watching it.

"What is your problem, Evonne?" Mama grumbled. Dad gave a half snore and rolled his head in our direction.

"I wanted to show y'all something I'm excited about."

I walked to the bedside lamp and turned the switch to brighten the room, then handed the lease to Mama. She put down her knitting and took it, already frowning at the words "RENTAL LEASE" across the top.

That frown was familiar to me. It was the same frown she'd worn when she opened the door the night I'd come home from Spelman; when I'd been accepted into Healy School of Beauty, when I'd been offered a chair at the Curl & Dye, and when I launched my website.

"What have you got yourself into, that we're gonna end up paying for?" Her eyes darted down the page, then she quickly flipped through them, grunting at my signature on the last page.

"What's it look like?" I laughed, but Mama's face said she wasn't in on the joke. Or… she didn't find the matter to be a joking one. "I found a cute spot in Potter Lake, and I'm moving out there. The rent is affordable and--"

"How are you going to pay for this place, Evonne?" Mama shook her head, flipping through the pages again. Her eyes settled on the amount of rent I'd be paying.

"I work, Mama. Two jobs."

"You don't work no two jobs," she argued, shaking her head. "Looking at the internet is not a job."

"Alright, I have *a* job; it's steady, and it pays, plus tips. I can afford this place on that job alone. I've appreciated being here while I got myself together, but I'm coming up on thirty. It's time I did for myself."

"So you planned on living here, using up electricity, food and water, space and saving your lil' coins all this time. And when I need help with Emmet and Edwin, and your grandmother is old and feeble, you're jumping ship. To do for your-self, you say."

She frowned harder and hit me with her patented glare. "Some children are just selfish," she mumbled under her breath.

"Mama, you still have Ebony. She can do a lot more around here. That girl is going nowhere unless some man proposes to her."

"We're not talking about Ebony! Ebony has a job."

Incredulous, I rocked back on my heels and planted my hands on my hips. "So do I!"

"You do hair for a living, Vonne. In a lil bitty town full of old people. Are you telling me you can live on your own doing old people's hair? Girl..."

She shoved the papers at me. "Here. We don't have any money to help you, so don't ask. Do you know how much money—"

I rolled my eyes to the ceiling, finishing her sentence. "... you wasted sending me to school... I don't see how I could ever forget that debt because you remind me every time I do something you don't want me to do."

"All that money for you to get kicked out!" She shot back, aiming her needle in my direction.

"I didn't get kicked out, Mama. I got suspended—"

"It's the same thing, Evonne!"

"No, the difference is that I could have gone back, but you *made* me quit because you were too embarrassed to fight for me." I folded the lease again and clutched it in my fist. "So, yeah. I'm moving out, and I don't see how there's much you can do to stop me."

I flipped the lamp off again and stormed out of the room. I was down the hall and headed toward the basement steps when I heard Dad ask, "Who's moving out? What was that about?"

Things had been tense since that night, but I made an

effort to double down on my responsibilities. I got up extra early to clean bathrooms and start laundry, got the boys' uniforms for the week ironed and hung, did the grocery shopping, and refilled prescriptions for Grandma Bobbie.

At night, I came right home from the salon and got in the kitchen, helping to finish dinner, set the table, get the boys to their seats, and cleaned up after the evening meal.

After all of that was done, I shot and edited videos, wrote blog posts, answered email, and did research well into the night.

Even Ebony, who should have been overjoyed that I wouldn't be ranting about cleaning up her side of our bedroom and bathroom, seemed sullen. Despite her negativity, she helped me cart my things to the small truck I had rented. The house was furnished, but I had boxes of wigs and hair accessories, not to mention clothes and shoes.

Ebony followed closely behind me in the rental truck while I drove the rest of my belongings in my car. I pulled into the driveway, and she parked behind me, then hopped right out with her mouth wide open. I could understand her reaction— the house was a beautiful stone stucco with huge windows facing the street.

"This is what we're doing now, Vonnie? This is how we livin'? Started in the basement, now we *here*?"

"The owner said he left the key in the mailbox. Let's grab them, and I'll give you a tour."

"Oh, he's a he, is he?" Ebony followed. "He's probably rich, too with this big ass house. Living here all by his lonesome. Have you met him?"

"Not yet. He's a doctor or something, so I'll probably never see him."

"A doctor? If you don't snatch him up, I will."

I reached into the mailbox and felt hard metal. I pulled out a set of keys and shook them in Ebony's face. She frowned and swatted them away. "The lease said the house was owned by some holding company, so I don't even know his name."

"I hope he's nice. You know, not one of those *thinks he's God* assholes."

"Me too, considering he lives so close. As long as he stays on his side of the property, we'll be good."

"Unless he's cute. Then he can be on *all* of the property if you know what I'm saying."

I took the path along the outside of the house toward the front door. It was standard white metal, but it felt like the entrance to freedom to me. I inserted the key in the deadbolt and then the knob lock and swung the door open.

A scent hit my nose, something light and clean. After walking around for a few minutes, I found the source: air freshener plug-ins, *Clean Linen*. A small bouquet of bright yellow and white daisies sat on the kitchen counter, along with a brief note: *Welcome Home. We'll meet soon.* —TW

I loved the friendly gesture. My landlord and I were going to get along fine.

I set the note down and turned a full revolution, taking it all in. Ebony walked through the place, swooning at everything from the picture windows to the view of the backyard.

"Ooh, Vonnie! You can do your videos here!" She dipped into an alcove space off of the kitchen. It was almost a room, the perfect amount of space.

"Yeah, I thought that would be a good spot. I'm going to get something to dress up the back wall. I'll do those open bookcases for products, and display stands for my wigs. I can mount the ring light on this wall," I tapped the wall nearest me. "And I'll set up a shelf for the camera to sit. I can edit the videos anywhere, so I'll probably do that—"

"Hello?"

A rich tenor that I hoped wasn't attached to someone standing inside my place called into the house. I glanced at Ebony, eyes wide. She bounded out of the alcove.

"Eb! Wait—" I wanted to grab her, in case it was a serial killer who haunted small towns and kidnapped cute black girls.

"Hey. We're back here." *Brilliant, Eb. Tell him exactly where to find us, chop us up and bury us in the backyard.* "Who's there?"

Footsteps sounded on the tile just inside the door. "Hi. I'm here for Evonne."

I followed her around the corner. "Way to tell a stranger exactly where we are, Ebony. You know that's how that girl got murdered on last week's episode of The Butler Did It."

My eyes sought out anything I could use for a weapon if I needed it. But then I realized that I wouldn't. Need a weapon, that was.

Because I knew the man that was standing in my kitchen. I could never forget those soulful eyes, gorgeous dark skin, full lips. The blue scrubs that seemed cut to fit him precisely, the way they stretched across his chest and cradled his arms in such a nice way.

"Nurse Dude," I finally said, when I could find my voice. He was such a pleasant sight, considering that he was probably not a serial killer.

"Miss Girard."

"Nurse Dude? Miss Girard?" Ebony repeated, swiveling her head from me to him and back. "You know him?"

"I-I-I...how... what..." I stuttered, then shook my head to arrange my thoughts and cajole my mouth into forming a complete sentence. "This is my new place. Do you live close?"

"Yes, I'd say I live close." He laughed, showing all of his teeth. "I own the place. I left you the flowers and the note... I'm—"

I snapped my fingers and pointed. "TW! Taj Wright, Registered Nurse."

"The one and the same," he said, nodding modestly. "I intended to be here when you pulled up. I don't normally work day shift, but I switched so I could be here. We had a last minute walk-in and—"

He waved a hand, then tugged at the hem of his scrubs. "So, welcome. Let me know if you have any questions. And you'll want to pull the moving truck into the driveway. It sticks out into the street and the neighbors..."

He hummed, wagging his head side to side while rolling his eyes. "I'm not leaving again tonight, so use my space."

"Ebony?" I hinted, since she had the key to the truck, but she stood there, her hands propped on her hips, and her chest pushed up and out. "Ebony! Go move the truck!"

"Oh, right!" She pulled the key from her pocket and teetered out on her stilettos. "Be right back!"

I moved into the kitchen and leaned against the counter in front of the dishwasher. The scent of the air freshener hit me again, and I realized that he had been inside my home. It didn't feel like a violation, considering the house belonged to him. It was weird, though, knowing that he had set things up for me, bought flowers, wrote a note.

"So..."

"So..." He mimicked, moving around the outside of the kitchen, leaning a set of meaty forearms onto the counter, muscular without hulking out like an NFL fullback.

Whew. Was I going to be living mere feet from him? *Look at God.*

"So..." I repeated, wishing I had a bottle of water because my survey of him had me parched. "You didn't think you should let me know that you are TWM, LLC, the holding company referenced on the lease? And that you own this house and would be renting to me? And that it was the same you that treated me at the clinic?"

He shrugged strong shoulders and smirked. "I put the house under my LLC for tax and privacy purposes. And there's no law that says a nurse can't rent a house to a former patient. Speaking of—"

He straightened, stretching out his arm. "Let me examine that cut. You didn't come back to the clinic and let me check it out."

"Oh…" I clutched my still-tender hand to my chest. "No need. It's fine."

"Then let me see it."

"It's okay. You did a fine job."

"Then let me see it. Didn't it heal?"

"Is this what it's going to be like? You coming down here to randomly check me for a fever?"

He laughed, dropping his hand. "Not at all. I take that very seriously. I only came in tonight because the door was open and someone was here to tell me to come in."

"In the future, don't do anything Ebony tells you to do. She has ulterior motives. She plans to kidnap you and make you her sex slave or Sugar Daddy."

Taj laughed.

"Wait until you find out I'm only halfway kidding."

He laughed again, so hard this time that the corners of his eyes crinkled up. "So… well, I'll let you unpack and get settled. I came down to tell you about the truck. It would be a terrible way to meet the neighborhood busy bodies." He moved toward the door, talking as he walked. "Let me know if you have any questions. My cell phone number is on the lease, so call any time."

But suddenly I wasn't ready for him to leave. "Hey, if you want to check this," I offered, waiving my injured hand in the air. "For checking's sake. It does still hurt."

His brow furrowed. He came around the counter toward me and immediately cupped my hand in his. He was warm, and his skin was soft. He'd been wearing gloves when he treated me.

"Any sharp pain? Like a stabbing feeling or throbbing?"

"More tender, not constant throbbing pain. But if I press

on it—" I did so, then flinched, sucking in air through my teeth.

"Well, then don't do that."

He peeled back the bandage and inspected the progress. "*Hmmm*. It shouldn't be this red, but it could be irritated by using the hand a lot. Try to give it a rest tonight and leave the bandage off. Let it breathe. Let's see how it looks tomorrow. It seems to have closed up fine."

"You think I'll have a scar?"

He peered closer, tipping his head one way and then the other. "Hard to tell. Why?"

"They're often on camera, so—"

"Camera?" His eyes rolled up, meeting mine. "Will you be shooting any low budget films?"

I laughed, yanking my hand back from his grasp. Then regretted doing so, not from the twinge of pain but because he was so warm. "I have a web channel. *Hair by E.* I do beauty and hair reviews and stuff. Aside from that, I need to be able to use both of my hands at the salon."

"You should be fine, Miss Girard. But let me know if you need a referral to a plastic surgeon." A beautiful brown lushly lashed eye winked at me.

"See, there you go. Giving me shit."

He laughed. "You make it so easy."

"If y'all are done flirting," Ebony interrupted, a large box labeled WIGS, 1 of 4 in her arms. She didn't seem amused at how close Taj stood to me or how friendly we seemed to be toward each other. "We need to unload that truck, so I can return it tonight. I'm not letting my car sit at the rental place all night."

"I'll let you get to it. Holler if you need anything." Taj sauntered out of the kitchen and out of the front door, pulling it closed behind him.

I made a half-turn, trying to decide where to start. "That box is wigs, so let's start a stack along that wall." I pointed toward the hallway leading to the alcove. Ebony smirked, slowly sauntered past me and set the box down, then pushed it against the wall.

Then she turned to me, a hand propped on one hip. "Nurse. Dude."

"Don't start, Eb. I'm going to grab some boxes. Did Daddy put his dolly in the truck?"

"Nuh uh, Vonnie." Stubborn, she folded her arms across her chest and planted her stance, her head tipped to the side. "You weren't going to tell me about the super cute chocolate nurse with the face and the arms and the chest and the eyes and shit? And how he lives *next door?*"

"He was my nurse at the clinic the night I fell, Ebony. He bandaged my cut, that's all."

"Had to be more than that. Y'all got nicknames for each other. *Miss Girard.*"

I rolled my eyes to the ceiling, noting the beautiful, hand-cut wooden fan for the first time. The design details in the house were impressive. "I flipped him shit. He flipped it back. He happens to own this house, which I told you I didn't know when I rented it. Can we unload this truck now?"

"Fine. But expect me to be out here visiting a lot. I might need a lot of personal health care from your landlord."

seven

. . .

EVONNE

"Alright, Sage. Let us know if Bennett can keep his hands off of you with this new look you got goin' on."

I gripped the back of the salon chair and spun it around so my client could see my handiwork. I put a little extra kick into it today. She'd asked for something fresh and young but not too young, and I felt like I'd delivered that with a close shave around the sides, leaving plenty upfront and on top for a flirty bang.

"Oh, now this is cute," she crowed, turning her head from one side to the other. I handed her a mirror so that she could see the back. "Ooh, the line in back is so sharp."

"You wear that well, Sage," said Leslie from across the salon. "Evonne is so good at creating styles that fit the face."

"Uh huh, I see that. It's sassy, but age appropriate. I like this. I really do."

I beamed with pride when my clients were happy with their hair. Even prouder when my bosses were happy, too.

Now that I lived on my own, I was under pressure. I had to prove to Mama that yes, I could make a living doing hair.

"I love it when I can put a smile on your face. I hope Bennett is taking you someplace nice to show off that new hair. I want a lot of people to see my work."

"We're going to Zucco for dinner. Bennett's gonna think he got a whole new woman."

"He won't know what to do with you. You need some work on your brows, and you can get out of here."

Sage peered closely at her face in the handheld mirror. "My daughter said I have brows like Bert from the Muppet Show. You sure keep an old lady feeling young, and I appreciate that. So does my man."

"You're what? Forty-eight? That's not old, Sage." Leslie was applying a silver rinse to Cara Isaacs, a salon regular. She talked, waving a brush caked with product in the air. "At least I hope it won't be when I get there. And even if it were, it wouldn't matter. Look at Earline, getting ready to marry the Colonel."

"Oh, how are the wedding plans going?" I asked. I tipped Sage back in the chair so that I could work on her brows. "She must be so excited."

Leslie gave a short snort of laughter. "She is beside herself, got wedding magazines sitting out everywhere at City Hall. Over the top about everything. You'd think she was the only person over sixty to get married."

Sage laughed, careful not to move while I worked a long thread across an already well-shaped brow. "Knowing Earline, she thinks she's the only one that counts. I'd be excited too if I were her. I was alone for five years before I met Bennett. She's been single a long time, I hear."

"Mmmmm," Leslie hummed. "I was little when her husband died. It was a building collapse, I believe. I barely remember him. They'd been together since they were teenagers. She said she felt like she could never love again. Then along came the Colonel."

She chuckled, smoothing the tint through Ms. Cara's hair while the salon listened. "She said, watching me and Kade gave her hope, and that warms my heart. *A little*. She's still a gossipy old woman, in everybody's business."

The shop erupted in laughter so loud that, with the background music going, none of us heard the door swing open. It wasn't until a male voice called out, "Excuse me?" that any of us noticed someone had come in.

At the front of the shop, looking good enough to eat in a thin, long-sleeved striped sweater and dark blue jeans slung low on his hips... was my landlord.

When Taj said he worked odd hours, he meant it. I hadn't seen him since I'd moved in. I heard the garage door roll open at various times, mostly well into the evening. He never stopped by to say hello, never popped by for no reason.

Much to my disappointment.

"Hey!" I waved a pair of tweezers at him, catching his attention. "This is a surprise. You want your brows done?"

He grinned, showing off blinding white teeth. The man must sleep in Crest Strips. "I heard someone named Tamera gives a great cut. Thought I'd stop in for one."

Leslie and I pointed at Tamera, whose chair happened to be empty. She propped a hand on her hip and looked him up and down. He didn't seem disturbed by the scrutiny. "You're sure you don't want to be at Guys N' Dolls, across the lake? They do men's hair over there."

"I went there, and the chairs were full, and so was the overflow line. The manager said if I wanted a good cut to come over here and ask for Tamera. Are you her?"

"Unh huh. That's me."

Tamera grabbed one of the new black capes with the bright white Curl & Dye logo and motioned Taj toward her chair. He slid into it and sat back, watching the satin float on air and settle onto his form. "You like anything in particular? You want your goatee touched up, too?"

"Keep it simple," I heard him answer. "I don't have time to hit the barbershop every week, so I want to keep it looking fresh for a minute. Line it up, make it nice."

"I got you."

With a flick of a finger, the air filled with the sounds of hair clippers and Janelle Monae. Typically, this would signal another round of salon talk, but the shop was suddenly devoid of chatter. It was so unusual; it made me uncomfortable.

Leslie sent Ms. Cara over to the hairdryers and got her set up under a hood. She pulled a magazine from her bag to flip through. Or pretend to flip through, because she had come to love beauty shop gossip as much as any of us.

Leslie tapped Taj's knee as she passed Tamera's chair. "What's your name, young man?"

"Uh...well, I don't know about that young man stuff. From what I hear, you and I aren't too far apart, age-wise. But my name is Taj. I work over at Lakeside Regional Clinic."

"*Ohhh*. Okay." She nodded, keeping busy with mundane things that she didn't have to do, but did just to stay in his face. "I didn't realize Doc Moore was bringing in such young blood. What's your specialty?"

"Specialty?"

"Cardiology? Pediatrics? Internal Medicine?"

I watched Taj's facial expression change with his effort to contain a sarcastic comment. I didn't know him well, but by now, I knew what that face meant. I busied myself with cleaning my station and prepping for my next appointment. Angela would be coming in for her monthly ritual; a wash and roller set, round brush blowout, facial, brow threading, and mani-pedi. She would be the last client of the day.

"Actually," he replied, "I'm a *nurse* at Lakeside. I did a

tour when the clinic was under construction. I was impressed. I applied when they started adding staff."

"Oh… a male nurse. Well, aren't we progressive, at Lakeside!" Leslie wasn't even pretending to work anymore. She sat in her salon chair and crossed one leg over the other. "So, you live here in town, then? When did you move here? Did your uhm… *family* move with you? I've just never seen you around. You're not on the basketball league or anything?"

"I live close to the clinic, that side of town. My family is back in Jacksonville, so it's just me. I've been busy buying my house, renovating, decorating… getting settled in. I pretty much just work."

Taj pressed his lips together as if that put an end to the discussion. He didn't know the stylists at the Curl & Dye. A discussion didn't end until they were ready for it to end.

"Buying a house. Renovating. Decorating. Mmmhmm…" Leslie turned her head toward me and gave me the silliest grin. I knew what she was doing.

Tamera flipped the clippers off, picked up a different unit, then flipped them on, this time bending close to his face to fine-tune the line of his goatee. "Do not move, or this won't be right. You can't walk out of here looking wrong. I have a reputation to uphold."

"And so… Evonne, how do you know Taj?" Leslie pressed.

"He was my nurse at the clinic, the night I fell during that storm. Fixed me right up." I showed my bandage-free hand with the tiny scar that couldn't be seen, as he'd promised.

Tamera hung the clippers in their slot, then used a brush to remove loose hairs from his neck. Then she handed Taj a mirror so he could inspect her work. It wasn't anything intricate, but it was super sharp. The way he grinned when he saw himself, taking in the view from one side and then the other, he must have agreed.

"I cut it close so that it won't be out of control in a week. You come back and see me when you're ready for a refresh."

"I think I've found my new barber," said Taj, then gave a low whistle. "Unless..." His eyes flicked up to mine, and that sarcastic half-grin flashed at me. "You make house calls?"

I grabbed a pair of oversized scissors and snipped them in his direction. "Sure! I'll bring these home and fix you right up."

The moment those words left my mouth, I knew I'd messed up. Tamera and Leslie exchanged a knowing glance between them, but neither said a word. Tamera removed the cape and shook the loose hair from it, then hung it over the back of her chair, lowered the pump and gave Taj a tap on the shoulder.

"Front counter. I'll ring you up there." Taj followed her, produced a card when she told him his total and tucked the receipt into his wallet when she handed it to him.

As soon as the doors closed and we'd all watched from the window as he climbed into a jet black Mercedes, both Leslie and Tamera appeared at my station, arms crossed. I glanced around them, hoping the door would swing open, and Angela or *anyone* would walk in.

Nothing. The door stayed shut, and those two stayed in my face, and Ms. Cara was bent over sideways, trying to eavesdrop.

"Home?" Tamera asked, one eyebrow cocked high.

"Something you're not telling us about Taj?" Leslie asked.

"It's not what you think." Nervous for no reason, I grabbed a few items from my cabinet and began setting them out for Angela's appointment.

"Well, then what is it, honey?" Ms. Cara called from across the room.

"You holding out on us, Evonne?" Tamera asked.

"Because you seemed to know him," added Leslie. "And he seemed to know you."

"And I'm going to ask again, in case you didn't hear me. *Home*?" Asked Tamera.

I feigned anger, throwing a discarded apron into my salon chair. "Damn, y'all are nosy! Taj owns the house I live in."

"Live in..." Tamera repeated. "So, you two are living somewhere together in the same house?"

"I rent his guest house. We share a garage, and there's an entrance to the house from there. Otherwise, it's a completely separate space."

I glanced from Tamera's face to Leslie's and back. "Seriously! I said I hadn't met my landlord and that it was a company name on the lease—"

"But now it appears that you have," Tamera interrupted. She slowly turned, heading back to her station. "He wasn't wearing a ring. Not even an indent like he had one and took it off. So is Taj... available? Know what I'm saying?"

I blinked, flustered. "I don't know. I've never seen a woman or another car at the house." I shrugged.

Leslie hummed, tapping two fingers on her chin. "You'd have seen a woman if he had one. She'd come around. Mark her territory, make sure you know he's not on the market. There's no way a woman lets a man that *fine* rent his guest house to a young, single woman. Certainly not if she'd ever seen Evonne."

She returned to her chair, but not before issuing a warning. "Be sure to keep us posted on important developments, Evonne. And don't leave anything out. I've got my eye on you, little secrets keeper."

"He's my landlord, and that's all. There won't be any developments."

"He was giving quite a few lingering glances," said Ms. Cara, butting in again. "I know an interested man when I see one. Do you want him to be *more* than your landlord, dear?"

"All right, it's not my business, but I detected a little

something between him and one of the nurses at the clinic. And you know how men in healthcare can be—"

"See how she deflects when she's the subject of gossip," Tamera teased.

"I'm not deflecting!" I argued, laughing. "I don't know what the big deal is."

"The big deal is that you were hiding some good gossip, and, in this shop, that's a sin." Ms. Cara closed the magazine she'd never read and tucked it back into her bag. The dryer had shut off, so Leslie motioned for her to move to the shampoo bowl. "Did I ever tell you ladies how I met my husband, Garth?"

She settled into the seat and leaned back. "He was my mailman! It was two years of *here's your mail* before he got up the nerve to ask for my phone number."

I was thankful to her for taking the heat off of me. I went back to prepping my station and trying to regulate my heart-beat. Outside of lusting after a handsome man, I hadn't given Taj a thought.

But now I couldn't wait to get home.

The salon door swung open, bringing with it the scent of early spring. Angela had arrived, wearing her usual tracksuit and pink sneakers. Since she was getting a pedicure, she carried a pair of flip flops in one hand and a cup from Rooster's in the other.

"Hey, hey! What's goin' on in here today?"

"Hey, Ms. Angela," I greeted her, grabbing her by the elbow and leading her to my chair before anyone could fill her in. I needed the shop to go back to its usual gossip about everyone but me. "Come on over. I'm so ready for you."

eight

. . .

TAJ

I pushed a grocery cart toward the fresh produce aisle at Pinkney's, not at all basking in the luxury of picking out my own vegetables. The Guys Next Door's last album blasted through my earbuds, and, despite myself, I bobbed my head to the beat.

Over the years, I'd heard stories from the guys about not being able to do everyday things like go to the grocery store, put gas in the car, or buy tools at the hardware store without being mobbed. Going to the mall was a disaster and forget going on vacation, unless it was to a private island or an exclusive resort.

I'd never known that life. I finished high school, went to college, worked my regular job every day. I floated around Potter Lake nearly invisibly while I completed the long list of tasks I saved for my days off. I wished that I was too busy, too important to do things like shop for groceries. I hated grocery shopping.

The music faded into the background as a phone call came

through. I glanced at my watch, swiping across the screen to pick up the line.

"Well, if it isn't the most beautiful woman I know."

"Unh huh. That's how I know you know you're in trouble. I haven't heard from you since last week. You could be dying of the flu, for all I know."

"Ma, I'm a nurse at a clinic. How could I be dying of the flu?"

"Nurses and doctors are the worst patients, and hospitals are full of germs. Besides, I don't know what it is you're doing out there. You go to other places than the hospital."

"I'm rarely anywhere but the hospital, but I'm actually at the grocery store right now." I picked up a bag of honey crisp apples, shook my head at the price and put them back. "The overpriced grocery store. You sure you don't want to come up every few weeks and do my grocery shopping?"

She ignored my question, launching into the real reason she'd called— to pester me about my health and get into my business. "How've you been feeling, son? Don't blow me off."

"I'm fine, Ma. I've been feeling fine. I'm busy, is all. I work a lot—"

"You know you need to be careful with working so much. Get your rest. Remember, when you got sick because of all of that running around—"

"Lymphoma is not caused by being busy, Ma. We've talked about this."

"I know." The same way I couldn't say the word remission for fear it would jinx me, she was uncomfortable when I called my cancer by its name. She preferred to say I was *so* sick, or *very* sick or just sick. She never said cancer. "I'm concerned. I'm always going to be concerned. Have you been in for a checkup?"

"I go for an annual checkup," I reminded her, though gently. "I'm current, and I'm fine. We do cancer screens every five years. You went to the last one with me in October. Remember?"

"I thought maybe since you work at a clinic, you might get checked more often."

"That would be convenient, but there's no reason for more than an annual check right now. But I promise that if I start feeling poorly, I'll ask the nearest doctor to examine me immediately. Okay?"

She sighed. Not out of relief, I knew. "There's no need to get smart. I'm concerned."

"Your concern is going to give me an ulcer. Catch me up on everyone. What are you and dad doing?"

I listened to her talk about my brothers and my father and everyone in the middle-class neighborhood that they hadn't moved out of, despite my offerings to move them. Dad was still Operations Manager at a paper plant; Mom still taught elementary school, and my little brothers who, at twenty-five and twenty-three hadn't been little in a long time, both lived close to my parents and were well out of school, trying to make it in their fledgling careers.

Distracted, I walked around Pinkney's Grocery, its wood shelves and concrete floors, and faded murals advertising "Co-Cola" and RC sodas a comforting throwback. I preferred the slower pace and the friendly faces over the bright, shiny ShopMart with slick linoleum floors and LED signs flashing sales on corn on the cob. I didn't prefer Pinkney's prices so much, but you take the good with the bad.

"I got a card for you from Ms. Doris at Jacksonville Cancer Center," she said, after her breathless update on everyone she knew. "She's finally retiring. They're throwing a big to-do for her at the Assisted Living center they moved her to. Won't that be nice? You should try to make it out here for that, if you can."

My mind rolled back to the early days of treatment at JCC. Ms. Doris, who called me Lil' Taj, was a stone faced, fast moving nurse that didn't have time for messing around. She liked her orders followed the first time, every time. I didn't think she liked me when I was first admitted. I eventually learned that she had lost a child to leukemia. She worked out her grief and kept her hands busy by becoming a nurse, then specializing in care for cancer patients.

"It's not you that I'm yellin' at, son," she told me one night when I was exhausted but awake and in pain. Ms. Doris had just finished raging at me about something innocuous. When I didn't react, she took a deep breath. She checked my IV lines and fluffed my pillows and tucked the sheets tighter up under the mattress— all the while, avoiding my pointed gaze. "It's cancer I'm mad at. Just workin' it out."

Some nights, after I'd sent my mother to a room to sleep, Ms. Doris would come to fuss and grumble, check my lines, try to get me to eat and stay hydrated and tell me stories about her son. "He was a troublemaker in his youth," she said, a missing tooth creating a prominent lisp. "Petty stuff. Shootin' off firecrackers in a field. Bustin' mailboxes with a bat. The boy liked to kill his Daddy and me.

"Once he got sick, though? That was my baby. We gave everything to save his life. He was my pride and joy; his daddy's too, God rest his soul. I had fourteen years with him. I wish we had more. You gonna have more, you hear me? You fight, cause you gonna have more."

Then she would roll her lips inward, bow her head, and stomp away until I rang for her again, or it was time for my next check. I couldn't believe she wasn't already retired, but Ms. Doris was the kind of nurse to work until they strong-armed her out of the front doors. And it looked like that was finally happening.

I forced myself to come forward. I tried not to live in that time too often, for too long. "I'll try to make it out for that. It's got to be way past time for her to retire."

"Well, good," Ma replied. "Then I can check you out

myself." She paused for a beat, then took a deep dive back into my business. "Anything else going on out there? Having fun with your time outside of work? You know what they say about all work and no play."

"Same answer as always, Ma. I don't get into much of anything."

"How about any*body*?"

"Ma!"

"Well! All of my boys are grown, and not one of you is trying to give me grandchildren."

I laughed so hard I had to lean on the handle of the cart. "You got to get off my phone, so I can get these groceries. I promise to call you more often to check in."

"Don't rush me off this phone. What happened with that young lady you said you met? At the clinic?"

I groaned, audibly. I already regretted that weak moment I'd had a few weeks ago when I told my mother about Evonne.

"She's my new tenant, is what happened to her."

"Okay. So, you should invite her over for a movie or something."

"Ma!"

"What? It's a movie, not a wedding. You never know."

"Ma, I can't date my tenant. It's... unethical. Or something."

"No, it ain't. You're punking out. Scared to make a move, because somebody might mean something to you."

"Ma, would you be serious? I can't—"

"I'm very serious, Taj. If you're okay, really doing fine, it's time to open your eyes and find somebody to enjoy this ride with. They say life is short, but it's actually a long time to be alone. You hear me, son?"

"I hear you, Ma. I have a long list of errands to finish, so I've got to go. Kiss kiss. Love you, buh bye."

I disconnected the call mid-protest. The music returned,

full blast. I checked my list, then my cart and my shoulders slumped. I had cereal, candy, and some pickles, but nothing on my written grocery list.

"I hate grocery shopping," I mumbled to myself, then redirected the cart.

———

Evonne was getting out of her car when I pulled into my spot next to her. Seeing my tenant twice in one day was a treat.

I'd done some snooping and checked out the web channel she had mentioned. *Hair by E* was funny and personable, a well-developed website with not just wig reviews, but tips on hair and skincare. The informed blog posts that accompanied each video emphasized quality content over shoving a bunch of buzzwords and poorly shot and edited videos onto the internet.

"*I'm E, signing off,*" she said at the end of each episode, which I knew because I had obsessively watched them all. '*Reminding you that you only get one body, so take care of it.*'

I cut the engine and pressed a button to pop the trunk.

"I don't see you for a week, and then I run into you twice in one day," she said, as soon as I climbed out of my car. "Making up for lost time, I guess."

"I was thinking the same. All done for the day?"

She nodded, leaning against the trunk of her car. I didn't know how women pulled off that casual, comfortable, *I make sexy as hell look easy* thing, but Evonne had it down pat. The clingy, fuzzy sweater she wore barely met the band of thick black leggings, which she wore with knee-high boots. She had a different hairstyle every time I saw her. The night I met her, she'd worn a short platinum blonde wig. The day she moved in, her hair was a shoulder-length crimson bob, and today was a cute spiky style with purple tinted tips.

"My last client always gets a lot done at one time, and it saps my energy. You must be off today."

"Yep. Errand day." I opened the trunk, ready to haul the bags upstairs in one trip, then wilted. Pinkney was using new grocery bags, which posed a new problem. "Ugh, these don't have handles. It's gonna take me forever to get them inside."

"Uhm, I have arms." She tossed her bag onto the hood of her car and stood next to me, eyeing the trunk full of brown grocery sacks.

"Oh." I blanched, my focus bouncing from the bags to her and back to the bags. I hadn't expected her to offer to help. "I'm just acting spoiled. Thanks for the offer, though."

"Oh, whatever," she grumbled, sucking her teeth and walking around me. She bent to lift a couple of bags, hefting one in each arm. "Stop being macho, Nurse Dude. Lead the way."

"If you insist. Thanks." After a few minutes of juggling bags and keys, I led her up the short flight of steps into the kitchen. "Set the bags on the counter, over there."

"Over... where?" She stood in the middle of the kitchen and made a turn. "You have four square miles of counter space in this big ass kitchen. It practically echoes in here."

I laughed, more at her tone than what she'd said. It was, indeed, a big kitchen. The budget for the kitchen was nearly as large as the budget for the rest of the house. I added a skylight and more windows, then pushed it out a few feet, taking up the space that was formerly the dining room. I cut the formal living room upstairs and used that area for the dining room.

"Yeah, it's a lot. I wanted lots of room for when family comes to town."

"How many people are in your family? You've got room for a small army."

"We are small in number, but mighty in appetite. And my little brothers are both bigger than me."

I gestured for her to set the bags down on the center island. "I'm going to grab the last two bags. Be right back."

I hopped down the stairs, grabbed the last two bags from the car and trotted back up, two at a time. Evonne had emptied one of the bags and was halfway finished unpacking another. My groceries were spread out along the counter.

"Hey. Thanks." I grabbed a can of black beans from her grasp and set it down on the island. "I'm very particular about my groceries. I go to Pinkney's because I can bag them myself. I do it in a certain way so I can unpack them a certain way, so I know where everything is, and—"

"Oh!" Her eyes grew big, and her mouth dropped open. Then snapped shut. "I am so sorry. I was on automatic. I didn't mean to take over."

"It's fine. I'm..." I watched her reach for the same can and grabbed her hand. "You're still doing it."

She laughed, then pointedly set the beans down on the counter. "I'm done, I'm done."

Her eyes flicked up and around the room, peeking around the corner as far as she could see from the middle of the kitchen. "I'm so impressed with your house. I would love a tour if you're okay with your tenant walking around your house. Oh, but you're doing your grocery thing. If you want to get all of this out of the way, I under—"

"How does anyone in your life get a word in edgewise?" She stopped talking, her mouth still open since I'd interrupted her mid-word. I extended a hand toward the adjoining hallway. "I don't mind giving you a tour. Shall we begin in the east wing?"

I led her through the dining room, where the table, a dark walnut with matching chairs except for white seat backs and cushions, was always set. I'd never eaten in the room; in fact, I only sat in one of the chairs at the furniture store. The centerpiece was a heavy crystal vase full of silk flowers, which matched the gilded framed photos of orchids and lilies that hung every few feet along the wall.

Evonne stood in front of one, her hands clasped like she was trying not to touch anything. "Did you pick these out? They're beautiful."

I shrugged a shoulder. "I don't do anything but work, so I had a lot of time to decide what I wanted, put rooms together. Besides," I said, gesturing to the prints, "these were on some overstock site or something. It's not like I bought them from an art museum or anything."

She glared at me, playfully so. "Nobody said I thought you got them from a museum. I said they were beautiful. Next?"

I strolled through the house, pointing out closets, a few random spaces, then rounding a corner into the large, sunlit room that faced the street. At one end of the room was my baby, the piano. At the other end was the entertainment center and a favorite feature— deep, plush suede couches with cup holders between each section that reclined at the touch of a button. Movies, basketball games, even the news could be viewed in maximum comfort.

"Wow," Evonne gushed, stepping into the room.

"Yeah, it's pretty cool down here. That TV is over sixty inches, plus I have all the little gadgets; you know, the Fire-stick, the HD antenna, the—"

"No, I meant this." She reached out, smoothing a palm along the glossy surface of the piano, then slipped onto the bench and flipped up the lid covering the keys. "You must play. Nobody has a baby grand that doesn't play."

I chuckled, rolling my eyes. "You'd be surprised. It's kind of a status symbol."

She held a key down and grinned at the long, clear tone that rang out. "What note is that?"

"Is this a quiz? Are you trying to see if I play?"

"Yeah." She pressed the key again, this time stronger. "What note, Nurse Dude? Or are you posing?"

I stalked over to the piano and sat, pushing her over on the bench. "That's F. And this is G." I pressed another key. "And this is C. And this..."

I danced my fingers along the keys in no particular rhythm, though my mind couldn't help creating a melody. "—is Taj Wright's Random Sonata No. 319."

She laughed. Like, cocked her head back and laughed hard, which made me laugh, too.

"Every kid my age took piano lessons, at least in my hood. You didn't?"

"Oh naw," she answered, sobering up some. "We didn't have a piano, so nothing to practice on. And no money for something like that. If it wasn't school-sponsored, we couldn't take part in it. Well, I couldn't, anyway."

"Do you have more siblings? Do they play?"

She nodded. "Edison is my dad's son from a previous relationship. Then there's me, and then Ebony, who is five years younger. She wanted to play flute so they bought her one. She lost it. Then she wanted to play the violin, so they got her one. She broke her bow, and that was it for music. The two youngest are boys, eight years apart. They aren't musically inclined, but whatever sport they want to be involved in, even if they suck at it, my parents are all over it."

"And you? They didn't believe in your artistic or athletic ability?"

Evonne shrugged. "I didn't show the aptitude or interest in it, so they didn't push it. I have always been able to do a mean head of hair. That's my skill. I guess."

"You can do more than that. You manage your website, right?"

"Well, yeah, but that's—"

"Being a webmaster is what that is. You write up everything on your blogs?" She nodded slowly. A crimson glow crept up her neck as she did. "So, you write, too. You film and edit your own videos. Plus, I saw that lady's hair today. You also do a mean head of hair. "

She nodded along, shyly smiling. Nobody gassed this girl up, ever. And it showed. "You're creative. An artist. Parents don't always see the value in that."

"That's for sure," she muttered. "Okay, Nurse Dude. You haven't proven you're not a poser yet. Play something for me."

"Tell you what. Scoot over. Real close, right here."

I tapped the seat, and she slid over, right up against me. I reached my left arm behind her and placed my fingers on the piano keys. "Lay your hands on top of mine, especially the tips of your fingers. And relax," I told her, feeling her fingers tense up, then loosen. I laid both hands on the keys, then adjusted her hands over mine. When I played, she would play, too.

"It'll be like you're playing your first piano concerto. Evonne Girard Sonata No. 1."

She giggled, then scooted even closer. Our fingers moved together from key to key, playing a song only I knew by heart. When I'd finished the song, I let the last note fade into the silence. She drew her hands back but couldn't take her eyes off of the keys.

"Taj, that was amazing," she said, her voice thick with emotion.

"So, you *do* know my name."

She started to laugh and tipped her face up to mine. At which point, I noticed that we were close. I felt her breath on my cheek. *That* close.

Since the night I'd met her, she'd been flitting in and out of my consciousness. I could *not* stop thinking about her.

I wanted to know Evonne.

It didn't take much to brush my lips across her full mouth. I hesitated before dipping back for more, in case she wanted to stop.

She didn't.

nine

. . .

EVONNE

Wheewww.

I was *so close* to throwing that man on the floor and riding him for all I was worth and then some.

That kiss was so good; I would probably dream about it, day and night. His lips were thick and soft— suckable, with not a hint of dryness. His tongue was wide and flat but wily. He flicked in and out of my mouth, teasing and tasting with ease and skill. He smelled heavenly and he felt even better, the way his muscles rippled when he closed his arms around me, when those big, warm hands roamed from my waist to my back, up and down and back again. My body was awake, and on high alert in ways it had never stirred for anyone else.

That sexy little groan that curled from his throat when leaned into him, trying to mash myself up against him....*oomph.* My thighs clenched and my pussy thumped just thinking about it.

But one of us had to have good sense. And since it wasn't

going to be Taj, I pulled back from a kiss that made him groan out loud and my temperature rise.

"We... should finish that tour," I quietly suggested. But not before I spent a few moments staring longingly at his lips. Because it wasn't that I *wanted* to stop...

This man was my landlord with a key to my home. Not to mention a lot of my personal information. He knew where I worked and where my parents lived. Taj had never given me a reason to fear living so close to him. I'd never have stayed if I thought I had anything to worry about.

But I was still paying for my last mistake. I didn't think the plan to become a cosmetologist was going to work, but it seemed to be panning out. Taking the full-time stylist position and moving out to Potter Lake both seemed to be right moves too, but I didn't want the Fates to have too much to deal with at one time.

So I did the sensible thing since it was becoming clear that if I didn't, Taj might let me fuck him. And I wouldn't be sorry about it, either.

When I hopped up from the bench, he did the same, his eyes everywhere but on me.

He led me to the other end of the room, where he mumbled about his entertainment systems. Built-in speakers and leather couches and remote control something or other. I was impressed but only half-listening. My brain was still buzzing with thoughts and scenarios of what could have been.

"Upstairs is bedrooms. A couple of guest rooms, bathrooms, and the master. I can show them if..." The end of the sentence trailed off. He angled his thumb toward the staircase.

"You can't leave me hanging, Nurse Dude. I've seen the east wing, the west wing... the dungeon." I chuckled. "I need to see the ivory tower."

Taj ambled toward the stairs and led me to the upper level

of the house. "I didn't have to do much to this level. I changed the carpet, added some paint and art. These bedrooms each have a bathroom," he said, walking me quickly past two fully furnished rooms.

"Closets," He continued, pointing at doors. "Upstairs laundry, which I didn't realize I loved until I had it."

He paused in front of a set of double doors at the end of the hallway. "This is my space. Like, not just my bedroom, but my *space*."

"Okay," I muttered. I caught a hint of reverence in his tone as he reached for the handles, turned them both, and pushed the doors open. He then motioned for me to go in first.

I anticipated a dark, masculine wood and leather man cave, replete with animal heads and things to grunt at. Instead, I walked into a cozy escape.

Plush carpeting underfoot, muted blue tones on the wall, and windows. So many windows. The far end of the room seemed to be for sitting. An overstuffed couch piled with pillows, and a light blanket was angled next to a stuffed bookcase and a small but elegant desk and chair. French doors leading to a patio that likely overlooked the backyard separated the two sides. At the other end, an enormous bed with a mile high padded headboard, flanked by nightstands, lamps, and an armoire, all in a light wood color rounded out the room.

"Wow, it's very blue in here," I commented, noting the walls, the shades of blue pillows carefully arranged on the couch, the midnight blue quilt covering the bed, and the lighter baby blue throw not-so-casually tossed across the foot of the bed. The pillowcases and sheets were bright white but the accent pillows were a dark blue that matched the quilt.

"Yeah. It makes me feel like I'm home." He shoved both hands in the pockets of his jeans, then pointed with his head. "Master bathroom is through there," he said, pointing at a closed door. "Other than the backyard, that's the house."

Taj's discomfort was palpable. Whether it was because.I was in his space, or because we'd almost crossed a line a few moments before and now we were in his bedroom, where we could pick up where we left off… or keep pretending that we had an innocent, landlord-tenant relationship.

Or maybe his groceries, still sitting in bags in the kitchen, were on his mind. Whatever the reason, there was such a thing as overstaying my welcome. I had to live mere feet from him and see him regularly.

"Your place is nice. *Really* nice. Like I could never even dream of…" I sighed, giving the room one last lingering gaze. "Anyway, I'd better head home. I need to film, and I want to catch some of this sunlight."

Announcing that I was leaving perked him up considerably, feeding into the feeling that I'd made him uncomfortable. He followed me out and pulled the doors to the room closed behind him.

Back in the kitchen, Taj propped his hands on his hips and surveyed the quasi mess, which was just a couple of bags of groceries sitting out on the counter and four full bags waiting to be put away.

"Guess I'd better get to work on this. It was good seeing you, Evonne."

"Yeah, you too."

I headed out the kitchen door and down the stairs. My bag was sitting on the trunk of my car, where I'd left it. I snatched it up and headed home, already mumbling to myself about not getting into a situation with Taj.

Well, any *more* of a situation. Because… it was already a situation.

ten

. . .

EVONNE

Taj was doing the most to avoid me.

If doing the most meant keeping the same schedule he'd always kept, where I only knew he was home if his car was in the garage. The garbage cans magically appeared on the curb on Friday mornings, and then made it back to the garage on Friday evenings, but I hadn't seen so much as a hint of a shadow in weeks. Though I'd hoped to.

I had a thin line of regret for not taking advantage of the opportunity that dropped itself right into my lap. I should have fucked him stupid.

We were adults—young, in the prime of our lives, attractive.

Attracted to each other.

YOLO.

I didn't blame him, though. I wouldn't volunteer to get mixed up with someone that lived next door. Besides, I was his tenant. And a former patient.

And I was pretty sure he had something going on with

that other nurse at the clinic, so I tried to put the whole incident out of my mind and get back to working hard at the Curl
& Dye and pushing my web channel to the top of everyone's
subscription list.

The day that storm came roaring back like it had been
riding a long rage boomerang changed everything.

It was Leslie's day to work at City Hall, so Tamera was
running the shop. She had one client that talked nonstop, and
on top of all of that noise, the radio blared. On a cloudy day, it
barely tuned in, and the light static under the music grated on
my nerves, so I organized with an earbud in one ear and
Giselle Gorgeous, my favorite beauty podcast, going loud
enough to drown it out.

A loud squawk over the radio waves made us all jump.

*'The Georgia Weather Service has issued a warning for severe
thunderstorms and heavy rain with possible flash floods and the
possibility of a tornado throughout middle Georgia. Residents
should seek shelter and stay tuned for further information as the
storm approaches. Affected counties include Bell, Crawford,
Hancock, Jasper—'*

"That's us," Tamera called out, pulling a roller from her
client's thin gray hair, then tossing it into a container next to
her. "If you don't have any appointments, you need to get out
of here, Vonne. Matter of fact, even if you *do* have appointments, you should go. Nobody's headed to the salon in a
storm."

I ignored her, going back to stacking products at my
station. I'd made some room, dumping containers of expired
creams or things I bought on impulse that didn't work like I
thought they would.

"It's just some rain," I told her. "And it's the middle of the
day. I live out here now. It's not a big deal to stay."

"They don't issue those warnings for shits and giggles.
We're not getting walk-ins in the middle of a rainstorm, so

there's no sense in hanging out here. I'm gonna finish up Mrs. Black and grab Erik at Guys N' Dolls."

"TC is not closing shop for a storm, Tamera."

She and I shared a knowing glance. KC's sister managed Guys N' Dolls and covered The Curl & Dye on occasion. TC didn't like to lose a dollar. Rain or shine, the shop was open.

"Well, I run *this* shop, and I'm out of here as soon as I'm done."

"You have to finish up anyway, so I might as well wait and leave with—"

"Why are you arguing with me, woman?" Tamera stepped around her chair and grabbed me by my elbow, pointing out the window at the storm already in progress. "See, it's already raining. You've got to go before it gets bad. I can't have you falling out in the parking lot again. Might get a wild hair up your ass and sue us."

"I'm not gon—"

"Get your bag, get your keys, get your butt out of here. Find a reason for your fine ass landlord to pay you a visit. See you tomorrow. Bye."

She marched me to the front door, opened it, and pushed me out of it. The door closed in my face, as hard as a door on rusty hinges that moved as slow as molasses could close. I rolled my eyes, feigned offense with my hands on my hips, then sneered at Tamera as she mimicked waving me away, then went back to Mrs. Black.

I drove home, which was so blissfully close, I could dance. I was proud of my little space, having added my own personal touches. Inspired by Taj's flair for art, I picked up a few pieces at a discount store in Healy and hung them. I kept fresh flowers in the vase he had placed in the apartment and made sure I had a pop of my favorite color, emerald green, in every room. A blanket here, a pillow there, glass canisters with a green tint.

My place was becoming more 'me' every day, and it was a

joy to come home to a place that, for the first time, was all mine.

The storm was raging by the time I got home. Raindrops hit like rocks on my windshield, and the wind blew so hard the trees bent in half. I flew through the short walk from the garage to the house, changed into comfortable clothing, then plopped down on the living room couch with a glass of Merlot and some snacks.

I spent the afternoon and early evening writing blog posts, editing videos, and listening to the wind whip around the house. I decided since I had some free time to work ahead and record a new review. I was an affiliate for a wig designer, and if I could have the video edited and up on the site before the weekend, I could have some sales.

I grabbed my glass of wine and went into my mini-studio, with silks on the wall, wigs on stands, products on display on a bookshelf behind me. I sat on a pile of pillows in front of a glowing ring light and a small camera with a chunky blonde and brown lace front wig in one hand, the other excitedly gesturing as I recited my pre-written script.

"Ladies, this unit is so cute right out of the box, but you know how I like to post photos of it styled and out in the wild, so check that out right after you watch this video. The cut is smart, and the texture of the hair is so realistic, it barely looks like a wig. Now, if you know what you're doing, you could cut this down into a short curly *fineapple*. Slim face, round face, triangle face...this unit flatters any shape—"

A sonic boom reverberated through the house so violently, the dishes in the cabinet rattled together. Seconds later, an almost daylight bright flash lit up the sky. And then, except for the red glow of the camera, the room was inky dark. The heat was off, and the air was still, the only sounds being the storm outside.

"Shit," I hissed. I set down the wig and stretched forward, pressing the stop button on the camera, more upset that I was going to have to re-record what had been a good segment than I was at a loss of power. I got up and felt my way along the wall to the hallway. The street lights must have gone out as well because it was pitch black outside.

I got to the kitchen and pulled a flashlight from a drawer. I clicked it on, and the tightness that had been building in my chest seemed to ease. I never did like a dark room.

In the distance, a door slammed. Heavy footsteps thumped, getting louder, coming right at me. Taj's spot had been empty when I pulled into the garage, but somewhere between my second and third glass of wine, I must not have noticed that he had come home. I was almost at the door when he began nearly beating it down from the other side.

"Evonne!" He called, yelling over the wind.

I pulled the door open, shining the flashlight in his face. Tree branches whipped in the air behind him, illuminated only by frequent flashes of lightning. And it was raining sideways, since the right side of his hospital scrubs were wet. He squinted, bringing up a hand to block the bright beam.

"Damn! What is that, a floodlight?"

"Sorry." I lifted my arm to aim the glare of the flashlight down on us instead of directly at him and stepped aside. "Come in."

He did so, uselessly wiping his shoes on the mat outside the door before coming inside, aggressively wiping his face with his palms. I reached around the corner and grabbed the towel that I usually kept hanging off of the refrigerator handle. He used it to wipe his neck and chin, capturing the drops falling from his goatee. He then swathed it across his clavicle and the small amount of chest that was visible in the V-neck of his scrubs.

I nearly swallowed my tongue. I felt like I'd watched Taj dry off after taking a shower.

"Thanks," he said, futilely dabbing at the soaked fabric clinging to his chest. "This weather is crazy."

"You've never heard that song, 'Rainy Night in Georgia'?" I reached for the towel, tossing it onto the kitchen counter.

"I know 'The Night the Lights Went Out in Georgia.' Never took either of them literally. Sorry if I uhm..." He surveyed me and my attire, swallowing audibly. "... woke you up."

I was wearing the bare minimum, as far as clothing was concerned; a lacy bralette under a midriff-baring sheer top that didn't do much to mask the ample bust that every Girard woman had been blessed with, paired with leggings that hugged every curve I owned, and there was plenty of curves to cover. Taj was trying, pretty hard at that, not to notice the skimpiness of my loungewear.

"If I had been asleep, I would have been fine, Nurse Dude. I don't need power to sleep."

"I just wanted to make sure you weren't sitting down here in the dark."

"What difference does it make? We're both sitting in the dark."

"I have a generator on the house." So he hadn't come down to make sure I wasn't afraid of the storm? I was slightly disappointed. "I have power, heat, and lights, too. I came to tell you to come upstairs. That is if you weren't sleeping."

"I was recording a damn video. The power cut out in the middle of it, and now I have to re-record it."

"Oh. Can you record it at my house?"

"My followers are nosy. They know my studio, and I don't need anyone asking where I'm filming from."

"Okay, then." Taj stood in the entryway, staring like he was waiting for something.

"Okay, then... what? Do you need to check the house or anything? You want to use my flashlight?"

"No, I..." He paused, letting out a little laugh. "Maybe I wasn't clear. There's no power down here. I have power in the house. I thought you might want to come up. You're more than welcome."

"Oh!" I laughed because he was laughing, but my heart was beating out of my chest. Go back to his house, where I almost threw him down and had my way with him, and he wasn't going to stop it from happening? "I thought I would ride it out down here. It's a power outage. It can't be too bad, right?"

He grimaced, sucking in a sharp breath through his teeth. "I think the transformer blew. The street lights are out; the neighborhood is dark. Potter Lake Power is twelve old men and a ladder, so it'll be a minute until they get us hooked up again. It's going to get cold down here. And then hot."

I considered this for a moment, sitting down here in this little house by myself in the dark.

For *days*. My shoulders sagged.

"Let me throw some stuff in a bag. I'll be right up."

"I'll wait."

"I don't need an escort, Nurse Dude."

"Maybe not, *Miss Girard*," said Taj. The irritation in his voice was amusing. "But you're independent and incredibly stubborn. You'll decide it's too much trouble and not come up. It's going to get cold tonight and hot tomorrow with no way to move air, and I don't want my tenant to freeze or bake to death in my house. It's horrible for resale value. *I'll wait*."

"You should listen to This Fly House. It's a podcast for homeowners. I've been listening to it, even though I don't own this place. Anyway, if the house is new construction, the insulation should keep me from—"

"Please." He clapped his hands together in prayer pose. "Would you *please* stop talking about podcasts and pack? Or talk while you pack? Or just pack?"

I muttered while I directed my flashlight back to the hallway to find my bedroom. "Fine. Even though the information could be useful to you."

eleven

. . .

TAJ

Inviting Evonne up to my place was unnecessary. Extra. Overboard. Not needed.

Kind and neighborly, sure. It was the sort of thing that Potter Lake residents would do for each other. I already expected the busybodies to make their rounds through the area, checking on every house to make sure residents were okay.

But I needed an excuse to see her.

We had nearly opposite schedules, so *'we live close to one another so I'm going to awkwardly, accidentally run into to you all the time'* would rarely happen anyway.

As soon as the door had closed behind her when she left my place a week ago, I realized that I'd probably made it sound like I didn't want her there, like I was rushing her out. That wasn't it, at all. I didn't know what to say to her, how to act after that kiss.

Having spent my formative years in and out of hospitals had stunted my growth, socially. In response to what women thought was an aloof attitude, they often took charge, so I didn't have to make moves. Like Jaslene, modern women went for what they wanted.

I'd never had to chase a woman. Evonne was the kind of woman I wanted to pursue. To flirt with. To get to know.

Yeah, she rented from me, but... we were adults, right?

As soon as I saw the bright daylight flash outside, I knew the transformer had blown. The entire street went dark, including my house, until the generator kicked in. A few lights flickered on, and the appliances that were tied to the backup power source cycled on again. Except, I remembered, the guest house was never wired to the generator.

I'd feel like a dick sitting in a warm, lit house while she was downstairs in the dark. And I suddenly had a perfectly good reason to bring Evonne and her scented hair products and smoky brown eyes and thick lips and winding curves to my space again.

Now standing in the hallway in wet scrubs, getting colder by the minute, I started to second-guess myself. I could have called. I had her number programmed into my phone, but it seemed so impersonal to ring her up from next door. Wasn't it more landlord-like to come down and make sure she was okay?

I heard drawers opening and closing and the muffled sounds of things, an awful lot of things, being dumped into a bag.

"Hey, you don't need much for tonight. You can always come down during the day and grab more stuff if you need to."

"I'm coming."

The beam of her flashlight announced that she was, indeed, on the way. I heard the wheels of a suitcase rolling across the floor. "I need to grab my laptop. Oh! And my camera. And the power cord to both. And maybe this wig..."

"Evonne—"

"I was drinking some wine earlier. Should I bring it up? It's already open, and I don't want it to go bad."

"If you want to. I have—"

"Okay, here." She shoved a couple of bottles of wine at me. One didn't have more than half a glass left in it. The other was unopened. "Take those. And carry this." She tucked her laptop into the crook of my arm. The other items were stuffed into the front pocket of her suitcase.

"You wanna uninstall the kitchen sink and bring that along?" I smirked in the glare of the flashlight pointed at my face.

"Why is your mouth so smart?"

"Why do you make it so easy? Let's leave this here." I handed the bottle of unopened wine back to her. "You can finish the open bottle. I have wine if we feel like we need some. No need to drink up your stash. Ready?"

"I guess," she mumbled, then walked past me to the door. I followed, laden down with her belongings.

It was raining, but the wind had calmed. It was still teeth-chattering cold, though, so we hurried down the sidewalk to the garage door. I slammed it behind us and followed Evonne up the steps, forcing myself to watch her feet in those furry, ugly little boots that girls wear and not on the entirely more attractive, shapely hips in my face.

"Door should be open," I muttered, steps behind her.

She flung open the kitchen door and marched in, parking her suitcase against a cabinet. I frowned at wet wheel marks on the tile, but I'd deal with that later.

"Make yourself at home. You remember the place. The important things work— lights, microwave, stove, water heater."

She dumped an armful onto the spotless kitchen counter. "The east wing, the west wing, the theater, the ivory tower." She gestured in each direction with her hands. "Where can I put my stuff?"

"I guess you'll be in the ivory tower with me," I said, grabbing the handle of her suitcase. I lifted it, so the wheels didn't mark up my floors. "Uh, Evonne? How long were you planning to stay? This feels like..." I lowered and lifted the emerald green monstrosity a few times. "Weeks."

"It takes a lot to be me," she answered. "I need all of my beauty tools and my cute clothes and shoes."

I led her from the kitchen through the dining room to the steps at the end of the hall. I paused once we hit the upstairs landing. "You can take any of these rooms but mine."

"That one," she said, pointing to the room next to mine. "This side of the house gets the morning sun."

"Yeah, I have blackout curtains so I can sleep past sunrise." I dropped her suitcase next to the neatly made queen size bed with a homemade multi-colored quilt and pushed a long, loud breath through my lips.

"You're so dramatic," she teased, then dropped onto the bed. "Am I your first guest?"

"Nah, I've had some dry runs," I answered, thinking about Jaslene. "I'll grab you some towels. Feel free to do whatever it is women do."

A few minutes later, I paused in the doorway, taking in the scene. Evonne's suitcase was wide open on the floor; its contents overflowed like it had exploded. Clothing and *woman stuff* covered the bed, and music blared from the bathroom.

I tipped my head around the corner. Evonne was at the sink, smearing something over her face and mouthing the words to Keri Hilson's *Pretty Girl Rock*. Her body rocked from side to side and, considering how tight and thin her leggings were, I'm sure that saw more than she intended for me to see.

Then she noticed I was standing there in the doorway, watching her like a creep.

"Too loud?" She shouted over the music, her shiny face angled in my direction. "I can turn it down. Gimme a sec..."

She stabbed at the phone with a knuckle until the music cut out.

I stepped into the room. There was plenty of space, but I felt like I was crowding her. I set the towels down on the counter. "I'll bring you a basket in the morning for the used towels."

She went back to what she'd been doing when I walked in.

"I've seen up your web channel, by the way. It's nice. You do a great job with it."

"Oh yeah? Thanks. I give hints and tips to men, too. Not like you need them."

I chuckled, not a hint of embarrassment. Good genes had given me great skin. I leaned against the wall, mesmerized by her movements. "What exactly are you doing?"

"What it looks like," she said, except it sounded weird with her mouth open. "Face massage. It's better with the fingers. I use this great cleanser, and I like to massage it into my skin. Really get it in there. Little circles with the tips of my fingers, for a couple of minutes."

Her movements paused, but only briefly as she took a long glance at my face. "Don't you have a skincare routine?"

I lifted a shoulder, then let it drop. "Soap and water."

She snorted, then went back to her massage. "Figures. I go through this process every night and every morning to look halfway decent." She turned on the faucet and splashed water over her face a few times, then reached for a towel to dry her face. "And you literally wake up like that."

She rubbed the towel under her chin and across her chest, dabbing her breasts. Her skin was clear, a flawless deep brown. Glowing. Dewy, I'd heard some women say.

I swallowed hard; I was sure she heard it.

"If I'm being honest," I started, then stopped. The question behind her eyes pushed me forward. "Well, and I don't mean to offend at all, but... you don't wake up so bad yourself."

She didn't respond unless you'd call staring at me with her lips slightly parted a response.

I took that as a hint that she probably wanted to get to bed and relax after the stress of having to temporarily relocate. I inched my way past her, out of the bathroom.

"Hey, Taj..."

I paused, one foot just over the threshold of the room, and turned. Evonne had come out of the bathroom, a mist of clean, fresh-smelling scent in her wake.

"You're not going to bed yet, are you?"

"Nope." I shoved my hands into the pockets of the damp scrubs I was still wearing. I needed to change; I was starting to itch. "I'm a night owl. And I'm off for a few days, so I'm in chill mode. You up?"

She scooted a pile of clothing out of the way and dropped heavily onto the bed. Her sigh sounded like it came from the center of her chest. "I'm a little jumpy. I've lived in Healy my whole life. We'd have a bad storm every once in a while, but lately, the weather is on one. I keep thinking about the last storm and falling in the parking lot..."

She shook her head. I nodded mine. That was the night we'd met. "You wanna hang out or something?"

"Well..." She paused for a beat, then an expression that read *fuck it* crossed her face. "Why not? Just because you're my landlord doesn't mean we can't be friendly. The rent is still due on the first, right?"

I'd been thinking the same thing. I was already doing un-landlord like things, like inviting my tenant, whose body I wanted to memorize by touch, to stay in my home.

"You can finish that bottle of wine you brought. I have another one I can open, and I'll whip up some snacks. Good?"

The way her face *glowed* and the relief that replaced her

worried expression, a small part of me hoped the power would be out for more than a few hours.

I could handle having a roommate if that roommate was Evonne Girard.

twelve

. . .

EVONNE

"Nurse Dude? Where'd you go?"

I stepped out of the bedroom into the hallway. The doors to Taj's room next door were closed, as always. The house seemed quiet. We'd said we would hang out, then he disappeared.

"I thought we had established that you knew my name, *Miss Girard*."

I poked my head over the landing and found Taj leaning into the stairwell and smiling up at me. "Nurse Dude is more fun. You need some help down there?"

"You can help me carry stuff."

I bounded down the steps and the hallway to the kitchen, where I found Taj being a regular Steven Homemaker. He'd finally changed out of his wet scrubs into a grey V-neck t-shirt and a pair of dark sweats. He stood at the counter, filling a large wooden tray piled with sliced meat and cheese, a few sleeves of crackers, and a bowl of popcorn. Two empty wine glasses stood ready to receive pours from an open bottle of fragrant red wine.

"I got this Grand Reserve Merlot from my realtor when I bought this place. Thought I should try it out."

"Grand Reserve? You're sharing this with lil' ol' me from Healy, Georgia?"

"Lil ole me from Jacksonville, Florida isn't fancy enough to be stuck up about wine." He poured a glass for me, then for himself. I lifted mine and we clinked glasses, then both took a sip. Taj swallowed audibly, eyes closed, then a low rumble came from this throat. "That. is. good. You like it?"

I nodded vigorously, taking a bigger gulp this time. Flicks of chocolate and cherries and a little bit of spice danced over my taste buds. Nurse Dude was going to turn me into a wine snob, and quickly.

He handed me the bottle and set his glass on the tray, then picked it up. "I'm not trying to be creepy, and it's fine if you say no, but do you mind hanging out in my bedroom? I don't want to put a drain on the generator by firing up the big TV and the entertainment system, because it takes—"

"Whatever has to happen for you to not go into a long explanation about power grids and whatever."

Taj smirked and cocked an eyebrow. "See, that's why I call you Miss Girard. Be careful with that wine. Dark red stains on my carpet are the stuff of my nightmares."

"Don't think I haven't seen you trying not to react to my stuff everywhere."

I heard him laugh, but try to hold it in. "I am an unrepentant neat freak, but I wasn't going to say anything."

"You haven't been holding back. You mumble under your breath every time I set something down."

I followed him back down the hall and up the stairs. He pushed the handle of one door open with his elbow and stepped aside for me to walk into the room.

"Mmmmm," I swooned. The room was cool and

smelled... *manly*. Yves St. Laurent-ish. "It smells so good in here. My brothers' room smells like ball sweat and feet."

Taj had flipped a switch when he walked in, illuminating the room in soft light. He laughed, setting the tray down on the small table between the loveseat and the fireplace. "I regret to inform you that there are grown men whose bedrooms smell like ball sweat and feet."

He picked up a remote and pressed a button. I heard a click and then saw a burst of blue flame. "The fireplace is gas, so we'll use that. Save some energy."

I plopped down on one end of the loveseat and set the wine bottle down next to the tray. I kept my glass, though, and took another healthy gulp. "This wine is great. I'll try not to drink the whole bottle."

"It's not the last bottle of wine on the planet." Taj eased onto the other end of the loveseat and picked up his glass. With a finger, he pointed at the tray. "Help yourself. There's plenty."

I did, loading up a small paper plate with a handful of salami slices and cubes of cheese. I snagged a few crackers as well, making a tiny sandwich of the ingredients.

Taj loaded up a plate with the same ingredients, except instead of crackers, he grabbed a handful of popcorn. "So," he began, then tossed a few puffed kernels into his mouth. After a few moments of chewing, his gaze settled on me.

But not regular looking, like strangers in a room making small talk. He *looked at me*. Like I was on display, on a stage, and everything was dark except the circle of light shining on me from above.

"So," I responded, crunching on more crackers to avoid returning his stare.

"So, I know a lot about you, understandably. You practically have to provide your life story when you fill out a rental application. But I don't *know* you, Evonne... what's your middle name?"

"I don't have one."

"You don't have a middle name?"

I shook my head. "Nope. None of us do. My parents didn't give us one."

"Hmph," he huffed. Then sipped more wine. "I guess I learned something new about you. My middle name is Anthony."

"Riveting," I droned. "So… I don't want to play this game."

"What game?"

"This *getting to know you* game, where you ask a bunch of questions and interview me like I'm in the running for some important spot in your life. We're neighbors. We're friendly, and that's cool. Let's just talk."

"Hmmm," he hummed.

A second later, he shot up from the couch and rushed out of the room. Just when I was worried that I had offended his delicate sensibilities, he walked back with a box in his hands.

"How about another kind of game?" He handed me the box and resumed his seat next to me.

I looked at it and laughed. "Okay, you want to get to know the vicious side of me."

He chuckled. "You say that like I'm supposed to be scared, *Miss Girard*. You in?"

"Oh." I flipped the box of giant UNO cards open and pulled out the deck. "Nurse Dude… I am *so* in."

———

"Draw four, sucka."

"Are you hoarding cards over there?"

Taj grumbled but pulled four cards from the stack at the center of the table, which we'd cleared off so we could sit on the floor and play our game. He had a hand full of cards that were hilariously huge, and neither of us was good at holding them, especially since we were both closer to drunk than tipsy.

We were three games and a whole plate of crackers, salami, and cheese in. I could see the bottom of the bowl of popcorn, and we were sharing the last of the second bottle of wine, a Stella Rose that wasn't as good as the Merlot but did the job of breaking the ice to bring out the trash talk.

We'd each won a game; Taj won game three. We decided game four was the championship, and I was playing like my life depended on it.

"I told you I was vicious." I gave him a reprieve and laid down an '8' in red, a color I knew was plentiful in his hand. The cards were too big, we were too close, and he was too loose to hide his stack.

Taj laid down an 8 but in blue. I happened not to have any blue in my hands. Nor did I have any other 8s. "You raggedy bitch," I mumbled, drawing a few cards off of the stack, finally laying down a blue card.

"See," he said, laying down another card I couldn't play. "What you don't know about me is that I'm a champion UNO player. Oh yeah," he added, nodding vigorously, watching me draw more cards that put me further away from the winning hand I had. "And in case you thought you were going to win..."

He slapped down a draw four and laughed hysterically.

"Maaaaannnn," I whined. I drew my cards and frowned. "What color?"

He called out blue. I played a card, and for a few moments, it was regular play. "You're too good at this. Is this the kind of thing you'd do with your family? Sit around and play cards and drink wine and talk shit?"

"More so with my brothers and my friends." He shifted his cards in his grasp. "My parents are into Dominos. Or Spades. You play?"

"Here and there." I played a card after Taj dropped a

yellow '4'. "I'm not good at it. My Grandma Bobbie taught me, and we don't get to play very often. My parents…"

My sentence trailed off as I realized that I didn't want to talk about my parents. I'd only spoken to Mama a few times since I'd moved out, and she was still unhappy with my decision, despite the fact that I was flourishing. Rent was paid, there was food in the refrigerator and gas in the car. My personal happiness didn't seem to matter to her, so long as I had failed to complete her plan for my life.

Ebony, who'd been out to visit a few times and who was always disappointed to learn that Taj was at work whenever she came by, told me that she'd started saving for a place of her own. Being 25 and still living under Rhonda Girard's thumb was no picnic, and now that I wasn't there to carry the load, she was starting to see the light.

"Your parents?" Taj prodded. "They don't do cards?"

I shook my head. "Have you ever met those super stodgy folks that think everything is demonic? Card games usually involve gambling, and that's straight from the devil. Concerts have dancing and popular music has suggestive lyrics, and that's definitely—"

"From the devil," Taj finished, laughing.

"That's why I'm grateful that I get to live here. Well, there," I corrected, pointing toward the guest house. "I get to be me. To figure out what I'm all about, away from them. Define what I believe in."

"You're what, 29? They held you down like that?"

"I don't know if they held me down. But I know it when they're disappointed. This is my second chance. You could say my middle name is Failure."

Taj paused, tilting his head. Studying me as if he could see the failure jumping out. "That seems incongruous with what I know about you, Miss Girard."

I laughed, shuffling my cards. We had stopped playing

and started talking, but I still intended to win this hand. "You can use SAT words all you want. It's still true."

"Okay… how so?" He consciously laid his cards down and picked up his wine glass. He moved around the table to my side. I did the same, picking up my wine and leaning against the stiff cushions of the loveseat. I angled toward him, my feet curled up under me. The gas fireplace had done its job; the room was toasty. But having Taj move closer ramped the heat up a couple of degrees.

"It's my dark past," I said. "I don't talk much about it, but I'm kind of drunk, so… fuck it."

"Yeah, fuck it. I won't tell your secrets. Deal?"

"Deal," I said, holding out a pinky. "Swear on it, Nurse Dude. This is for your ears only. Don't tell my shit. Don't even accidentally mention it when you're at the salon for your beard trim or whatever."

He looped his pinky around mine and pulled. "Deal. Now spill."

thirteen

. . .

TAJ

Before she could dive into her story, we got up off of the floor and moved to sit on the loveseat. I brewed a pot of coffee and poured us a couple of mugs, adding a few generous splashes of Kahlua.

Then I pulled out the big guns.

"What are *thoooooose?*"

Evonne's eyes hadn't left the platter of desserts since I'd brought them upstairs. I set it right on top of our abandoned UNO game, frozen in time but I was sure we would finish playing eventually.

"Drunken Donuts. Mini cake donuts drizzled in boozy glaze. It's a little spot in Jacksonville run by a friend of mine. We... we've known each other for a while. My mom drops in to buy a few dozen and sends me some every few weeks. There's vanilla with whiskey, chocolate with a liqueur and that one in the corner is my favorite— white cake with margarita mix baked in, glazed with tequila and lime and sprinkled with sea salt."

Evonne picked a vanilla with whiskey glazed donut and settled back with her coffee. After a few awkward moments and a little prodding, she started talking.

"Have you ever been kicked out of anywhere?" When I shook my head, she said, "I have. Spelman. Actually, I dropped out. After I was suspended; I just never went back."

"Okay. You didn't want to go to college?"

"I wasn't given a choice. I'd been groomed for Spelman. It's where my mother went. My father went to Morehouse. They fell in love, built a life. That's what they wanted for me. After the first semester, they stopped paying attention to me. I fell in with a group of girls. They were older, more worldly. I desperately wanted to be one of the cool girls. I started getting invited to stuff. And..."

"You don't want to say no, cause they're cool."

"Right. I wanted to be like them, one of the crowd. I let those girls lead me around like I had a ring in my nose. I did enough to stay on top of things and keep my folks off my back. And then—"

"Let's see... you probably met somebody..."

She nodded, rolling her lips inward.

"Very good! You know a lot about the college experience."

"And he was older?

"He was the older brother of one of the girls I hung with."

"And you were *so mature* but also *innocent,* and he was just drawn to you. Right?"

"Yeah," she whispered, head bowed, her gaze lost in her coffee. "He sensed my naiveté from a mile away. I loved his confidence. He was sure of himself. He had a way about him; he was charismatic."

"Of course. That's the game. He was probably not available a lot, right?"

"He traveled a lot. Every time he was back in Atlanta, he would call me. He made me feel wanted. He brought me things. He treated me nice. Well, I thought he was treating me nicely. I was barely living in my room if he was in town. If he was in Atlanta, I was living at his place."

"*Unnnhhh*. The sneak around. Things every college kid does." I took another swallow of coffee and nodded at her.

"He invited me to this party that *everyone* was trying to go to. A bunch of Atlanta famous people was supposed to be there-Chili from TLC, Jermaine Dupri, some Falcons players. He wasn't trying to hear that I was only nineteen, or that I was scared of my folks finding out that I was partying and not studying. *Everyone* was going. So, I went."

She laughed, dipping her head in mock shame. "What I remember was fun as *fuck*. It was in one of those big ass mansions. Then my date disappeared."

"Wait, he just left you there?" She nodded, humming the affirmative. "Oh, wow. How... how did you get home?"

"Well, I was a sloppy drunk, too young to be at this party, and I was pissed, screaming for him. Somebody told me that he'd left with some other girl. I went off, smashed a bottle into a giant fish tank. Somebody put me in a cab. Cabbie dropped me at the front gates."

"Oh. Well, at least they didn't call the police."

"So..." She held up a finger. "I'm wandering prestigious, historic Spelman College. Drunk. Belligerent. Campus Security rolls up. I assault one of them—"

"Whoa." I put a hand up to pause story time. "Excuse me, you what?"

"You. heard. me," she answered, slapping the beat of each word against her thigh. "I hit him. In the face."

I moaned, clapping a hand over my face. "Evonne...."

"I was a puny nineteen-year-old drunk girl. But it was all they needed to grab me up. I started screaming bloody murder and then... I passed out. Hit my head on the pavement, hard. They didn't know where to take me, so they called Atlanta police."

She paused, then dipped her head and added, "And the Office of Student Affairs."

I groaned. "Ooh, shit."

She pushed out a long, loud breath, then sipped a fortifying mouthful of coffee. "The Assistant Dean of Students at the time happened to be a family friend. She was instrumental in getting me to Spelman. *She* called my parents."

Evonne shook her head and rolled her eyes upward. "And because I had assaulted a member of the security staff, I wasn't allowed to go back to the dorms. I was placed on a disciplinary hold. My father had to drive to Atlanta to pick me up.

"I got my suspension papers in the mail. They didn't want me back until the next semester. My mother was *livid*. I thought we could fight it; it was my first real disciplinary action. My mother said that I had wasted enough of her time and money. I could sit on my butt at home since I didn't know how to act."

"And... the guy? You never heard from him?"

"Not since that night. If I saw him today, I'd punch that motherfucker in the forehead."

She popped the donut into her mouth and pointedly chewed, breathing heavily. By now, she knew everything about that guy had been a ruse to use her for her innocence, to take an impressionable young woman as prey and then toss her away. I didn't need to rub it in.

After a few moments, her hard breaths slowed, and she was solemn, staring into her half-empty mug of coffee.

"Every single thing I have done since then?" She lifted her head, tears delicately balanced on the rims of her eyes. "It's been ten years of trying to make it up to them, trying to be a good daughter and learn from my mistakes."

She swallowed hard. "They never meant to have me, you know? I heard Grandma Bobbie arguing about it with Daddy a long time ago. Mama got pregnant with me, and they were going to…. but for some reason, she didn't. Maybe she feels like I should have never been born—"

"I'm sure that's not it, Evonne."

"I can't think of another explanation for how she treats me, Taj!"

"Mothers don't think their kids are mistakes. You made some flubs, but what imperfect human doesn't? That was then; that nineteen-year-old girl is long gone. From where I'm sitting, I don't see a failure, Evonne."

"You hardly know me to know I'm not a failure, Taj."

"I know failure when I see it and…" I made a show of staring hard until she was giggling and hiding her face. "I ain't seeing it. I have perfect vision, and I'm a healthcare professional. I'm sure I'm right."

She giggled again, but the tears were gone, and I considered my job done. "So…it's your half of the pinky swear. Grab a donut and tell me your secrets."

I picked out a donut covered in a green glaze with large salt granules sprinkled on top. I wrapped my other hand around my mug of coffee and got comfortable. Then sat up again.

"Hold up. I want to show you something."

I reached past her to grab an old but well taken care of leather-bound photo album. I scooted closer to her and opened it, flipping past the first few photos stuck between clear pages. About halfway through the book, I slowed, then stopped. Then slid the album over to her lap.

She glanced at the photo. Then *stared* at the photo, mouth open. "Is this you? Are you in a hospital? You had a central IV line; that means it was serious." She peered up at me, any hint of inebriation gone, her eyes wide and wild and full of concern. "What happened to you? And are you okay?"

"I'm okay. When I was seventeen, I was diagnosed with B-cell Non-Hodgkin Lymphoma. It's the most commonly diagnosed type. Deadly if untreated, but a good many people that get a diagnosis make it."

"Oh my God…" She whispered, her words carried on the slightest of breaths. "How… how long were you…"

"A long time. Eight rounds of high dose chemotherapy and radiation. Then a stem cell transplant from my youngest brother. Then recovery. It was a few years until I was cancer-free. Even longer to feel like I was safe, in the clear. I keep things in check, of course, but I'm well. Despite my mother calling me every week to ask if I feel okay."

Evonne was, for the first time since I'd met her, speechless. She stared listlessly in my direction, but I don't think she saw me.

"I'm okay to talk about it," I prodded. "It's been a long time."

Her throat worked as she swallowed, then swallowed again, then glanced down at the photos of me at the hospital, doing my best to put on a brave face. I was thin but bloated, sallow, as pale as a dark-skinned boy could be. And scared to death.

She fingered the photos through the plastic, almost caressing my young face. "I feel like I was so close to never meeting you. It just hit me that I'm so happy I did. I'm so glad you made it."

"Would have been sad if I didn't, because Jaslene, my partner that night you came into the clinic? She had no plans to help you. You probably would have bled to death. Or got Gangrene, and your hand just fell right off. This girl I know heard about that on a podcast."

Evonne burst into laughter; the somber mood of the room instantly dissipated. She started flipping through the pages, smiling at photos of my family and me over the years.

"That girl, Jaslene. Are you and she *friendly*?" Evonne asked.

"Friendly?" Like I didn't know that question was coming.

I brought her up for a reason. "Like you and I, friendly? Or like friends who fuck, friendly?"

"Either. But mostly the latter."

"We have been both."

"Mmmhmm." She gave a single, resolute nod and flipped more pages, smiling at some of the photos of me with my brothers.

"What does that sound mean? Are you disappointed? Upset? Indifferent?"

Her eyes met mine long enough for me to see her roll them dramatically. "Definitely indifferent, Nurse Dude. I sensed something when I was leaving the clinic that night. You just confirmed it. She didn't like me."

"It wasn't about you. Not directly; she said I was flirting with you."

"You were."

"After I had turned her down earlier that night."

"Ohhh, ouch." She laughed. "Not smooth, Nurse Dude. No wonder she didn't like me."

"It's not like it matters. Does it?"

"Should it? Does it matter to you?"

"Not anymore."

She stopped flipping pages and turned toward me. "I'll bite. Why not anymore?"

"Because we aren't friendly anymore."

"Because you decided?"

"Because she broke it off. She wasn't happy when she found out who my new tenant was."

Evonne tossed her head back and let out a cackle that was more like a scream, replete with clapping and thigh-slapping. I might have let a chuckle roll out to laugh along with her.

"Oh-*kay*! I moved in with her man, and she wasn't having it!"

"I had already decided I didn't want to see her anymore. I told her that the day after you came through the house, and we uh..." I cleared my throat, searching for the words to describe the day I'd started daydreaming about my tenant.

Evonne had no trouble with the words, though. "Almost had sweaty sex on the piano?"

"I..." I paused, my mind speeding back to that hazy spring afternoon when I first tasted her. "Really?"

Evonne smirked, a saucy smile on her lips and smoke in her eyes. "Don't act like it didn't cross your mind, Nurse Dude. What happened when you told her it was over?"

"She accused me of playing games with her. She had suggested, a couple of times, that I should move her into that space. She was mad that I had decided not to do that. She threw some stuff around the supply room. Left in the middle of her shift."

I shrugged, splaying my hands in a helpless gesture. "I haven't seen her since."

"Disaster. I bet you're glad to have someone mature living so close to you."

"Oh, yes." I nodded. "Definitely." Then I licked my lips and leaned into her, eager to catch every word now. "Can we go back to sweaty piano sex? Really?"

fourteen

. . .

EVONNE

"Really," I popped back, but not with my usual bravado. Anticipation had erased the casual, giggly joking air and replaced it with a charged, more intense vibe. I was sending out attraction signals like Morse code, and Taj was picking them up, dot by dot.

"But you haven't... you don't seem... I mean, you've never..." Taj seemed flustered, waving his hands around.

"Busted up in here and rode you like a prize pony at the rodeo?"

"Okay, first of all, I am a mustang. But...yeah. It crossed my mind that day. And every day after that. Several times a day."

My eyes flicked up to his, hoping I would see what I saw in them. Lust. Desire. Need.

"Same. But I didn't need more than ten seconds to know you two had something going on. I like my men to be mine. And it would be awkward if things didn't turn out, and we still had to live this close to one another."

He hummed his agreement, his head bobbing forward and back. "Long, lingering glances across the garage…"

"Stilted, cold hellos, and goodbyes."

"Awkward…"

"Me seething when you bring all your women through here…"

"Wait… all what women? I don't have—"

"Or making a pest of yourself when I'm entertaining."

Taj splayed a hand across his chest in mock offense. "I resent the insinuation that I wouldn't be a mature professional in this situation."

"Mature professional? You made the first move, Nurse Dude. That wasn't very professional."

"It was a kiss, not a wedding," he teased. "Besides, I don't have a problem making the first move. Or the second one."

"Wait, what's the second move?"

"Same as the first move. Except we don't stop."

Taj leaned toward me, and because I'd been expecting him to, I tipped my chin, so our lips met in a tentative kiss. After a few moments of savoring the feel of his mouth on mine, he pulled back.

His eyes met mine, giving a seductively slow blink. "See? The second move."

"I thought the idea was not to stop."

I leaned in, and he took my lips again, this time with eagerness. My mouth opened, and the kiss deepened, the flavors of the wine and sweets and coffee mingling on our tongues.

I was already next to him, but I wanted to be closer. I rose to my knees, forgetting about the photo album still in my lap. It fell to the floor, landing with a thump.

"Oh. I'm sorry," I mumbled through kisses.

"Don't worry about it," he replied. "It's old."

Taj gripped my hips, pulling me forward. I settled on his lap, my body pressed against his. Through his sweats and my leggings, I felt him come to life, growing thicker, longer. Taj spread his legs and grabbed a handful of ass in each palm, tilting his pelvis up and grinding into me.

"You feel me? Feel what you do to me?"

I gasped, maybe even yelped a little, and returned the action. After a few moments, we were unabashedly thrusting into one another. His fingers crept up under the tank top and bralette I wore. Except for the thin pieces of lace and cotton, I was unencumbered, so his thumbs had no problem finding the beads of taut nipples and rasping over them.

I broke our kiss long enough to raise my arms over my head. "Pull," I ordered. Taj did as he was told, grabbing the hem of my tank top and pulling it off, taking the bralette with it. Now free, my breasts bounced between us; I *felt* the groan that ripped from his throat. A shudder rolled through him that came to me through his hips.

"Titties, huh?"

He answered, but not in words. Each hand cupped a breast, and he switched from nipple to nipple, sucking, licking bathing them until he was content, and I was at a near-scream, my hips crashing into his, trying to satisfy an urgent need. Taj was almost whimpering.

He wanted me. *Badly*. Knowing this made me feel powerful. It also made me want him more. I needed his body next to mine, his skin on mine. I grabbed for the hem of his t-shirt. He picked up on my hint and yanked it over his head with such ferocity that I heard the fabric rip.

I felt his hips rise, and in the next moment, he was standing, carrying me with him. My legs wrapped around his waist, and I held on for the ride across the room. Taj didn't miss a beat nor an inch of skin. He kissed and sucked his way to the bed and set me down gently.

I scooted back while he walked around to one side and pulled open a drawer on the nightstand. He brought a small white box to me, the brand NAKED emblazoned down the side. It was wrapped in cellophane and new, unopened.

"I want you to open them so you know you can trust me. No holes in condoms or tricky shit."

"Aw," I cooed, feeling oddly complimented by the gesture. He probably didn't ask Jaslene to open a new box of condoms every time they had sex.

I shook my head, pushing her from my mind. This was my time, I reminded myself while I ripped the wrapper from the box, then opened the top flap and pulled out a few individually wrapped packets.

"These say luxury condoms, Taj. You fancy, huh?"

He laughed, taking the box and tossing it to the side table. "They're good. Thin, so I can feel you, but not thin enough to break."

He stood in front of me, then nervously glanced around for a few seconds, like he didn't know what to do.

"You want me to do the honors?"

Without ceremony, he tucked his thumb into the waistband and tugged down his sweatpants, revealing himself to be fully erect and thicker than I had guesstimated.

Now *I* was the one whimpering.

My fingers shook as I ripped the package open and pulled out the latex ring. I took my time rolling it onto him, smoothing it down until he was covered, tip to base.

"All good?" I asked, rolling my eyes up to his, stroking him.

"All good. Real good."

He bent toward me and took possession of my mouth in the most passionate, groan filled kiss I'd ever had in all of my years of kissing men. While we kissed, he gently pushed me back until I laid on the dark blue quilt covering the bed. I barely felt him reach for the band of my leggings and pull them down, but before I realized it, I was nude, blazing hot and trembling with anticipation.

He dropped my leggings to the floor. And then dropped his head and buried his face between my legs. I almost shot up and off of the bed at the first stroke of his tongue across my clit, but I was too lightheaded to move. He hit a rhythm that was so good, I grabbed his head and pulled him into me, matching his tongue movements with gyrating thrusts.

"Oh... my... *fucking*..."

"Mmmmm?" He grunted. He seemed to be asking if I was good.

I... was so good. "*Shit*... don't stop."

As if he could since I had him locked between my thighs. And as if he wanted to, since he had a vice grip on said thighs.

There's a point, when I'm being feasted upon, that I know he's enjoying it as much as I am, maybe more. Watching someone approach that point always sends me over the orgasmic cliff. When Taj hit that moment— the rivulets of sweat, the deep skin flush, the rhythmic moans, the grinding of his hips into the mattress beneath him, I couldn't control the ascent— not the speed nor the ferocity, if I wanted to.

My legs fell open, and my head cocked back and I basked in the sensation of my own personal earth tilting on its axis due to a body-shaking climax.

Taj didn't waste any time, moving up my body. He pushed into me, working until I was full of him, until we were skin to skin, mixing sweat and air, grinning at each other like we were taking the other's virginity.

We moved against each other, tentatively while he learned my shape and what made me squeal. I discovered what made him shudder, what made his eyes roll back into his head. We did things to each other—base, erotic, primal things.

I had so much loud, wanton, delicious, then soft and sensual sex, over and over and over again, until a thin band of sun crested the horizon, and I collapsed in a heap.

With my landlord.
Fuck.

fifteen

. . .

EVONNE

I awoke to my cell phone chiming its usual alarm, but it wasn't in its usual spot when I blindly grabbed for it. The sound was muted. My eyes popped open like I'd been awake for hours. I sat up and glanced wildly around the room, searching for my phone.

And my bed, because this was not it. These sheets were too crisp, the quilt too soft, the pillows too... *pillowy*. Sunlight seeped around the edges of lined blackout curtains over the windows, keeping the room dark and cool.

Across the room, the snacks and glasses had been cleared. The only sign that we'd actually hung out there was the UNO game still in progress on the coffee table.

Footsteps thumped outside, then the sound of my alarm grew louder. A door burst open, and Taj stepped in, holding the phone and a set of sheets tucked under his arm.

"Rise and shine," he read from the screen. That's what I named my alarm. The first one, anyway. The second one, titled, *No Really Bitch, Get Up*, went off in twenty minutes.

I turned them both off and beamed a *thanks* smile up at Taj. He leaned toward me, coming in for a kiss, but I made a mean Keanu Reeves *Matrix* move and swerved out of the way. A hand caught my wrist as I scrambled out of the tangle of blankets and sheets and tried to duck past him.

"Where you goin'? I can't get good morning lips?"

"Taj, no…my breath is probably kickin' right now."

"Nobody's thinking about your breath, Evonne."

"I am!"

Taj, who'd obviously been up and moving long enough to take care of his morning ritual, laughed minty breath in my face. "Then close your mouth. You're not leaving this room until I put my lips on you."

I mumbled something about where else he could put his lips. He laughed and settled his mouth onto mine for a warm kiss. He groaned a little as he ended the kiss and pulled back.

Before I could utter a word, he placed his finger on my lips. "Aht! Aht! Don't. I already know you're about to say a lot about last night. Let's agree on something, okay?"

I nodded.

"Me and you had fun last night. And this morning. Right?"

I dipped my head again in agreement.

"I don't have a problem with you being my tenant. I like you, and I don't care. If you want to keep going, I'm game. If you don't, I'm square. No hard feelings, no macho emotions. Nothing awkward, no seething, long stares across the garage. At least on my end. Okay?"

I held up a finger, then ran from the room before he could grab me, dashing into the room I was using to dig for my toothbrush and toothpaste.

A few minutes later, I returned to find Taj standing where I'd left him, except he'd changed the sheets and made the bed.

I laughed loudly. "You can't help yourself, can you?" I

moved closer to him and rested my arms across his shoulders. "Now that I don't have morning mouth, I came to give you a proper kiss."

I rose up on to my toes and leaned in for a long, sweet kiss, savoring the taste and feel of his mouth. When we parted, I pulled back, studying the flawless matte that was his skin. "You should do a guest post on my blog—"

He groaned, pulling away despite my protests. "Let's get something to eat."

It took twice as long to get ready for work. Taj insisted on showering in his bathroom, which I didn't mind because it was bigger and fancier with double shower heads and slate grey tiles and white marble countertops. Mostly, he wanted to hop in and waste my time, pretending to help me soap up, instead making sure his lathered up hands touched every inch of skin and then some.

Then it took twice as long to get to work because the storm had ravaged poor Potter Lake. I swerved around downed trees, garbage cans in the street and low hanging power lines all the way through the main thoroughfare and across the bridge to the old side of town, which was even worse. Most of the homes and businesses on that side of the lake were older and less sturdy. People were outside, milling around front yards and storefronts picking up debris from signs that had been torn off of buildings and limbs that had fallen from trees.

I pulled into the strip mall that housed Curl & Dye and sucked in a breath. I could barely find a place to park, for all of the "pieces of building" that scattered the parking lot all from Ella's Boutique at one end to Larry's Ice Cream at the other.

Tamera, Erik, KC, and Leslie stood out front, talking with

two older men that I recognized as Leslie's father and grand-father. A few of the guys from Crawford & Sons leaned against a beat-up pickup with the store name in faded lettering along the side.

I parked as best I could and met everyone on the sidewalk in front of the shop. The front doors stood wide open, so I peeked inside and grimaced. It was worse close up.

The wind had ripped shingles off of the roof and some panels off of the front of the shop. Since the windows were old and brittle plate glass, they were no match against flying debris. At some point during the night, the wind had sent heavy pieces of wood through both front windows. With the rain and wind blowing in one direction and then the other, the shop had been rained on for hours.

I turned to face everyone after I couldn't look at the mess anymore. "It looks like a tornado came through there!"

Leslie tipped her head to me, arms folded. "Yep. It got us good."

"Are you and KC okay? How about Tamera? Your parents…"

"All fine," she assured me, nodding. "You and Taj okay?"

"Transformer blew on his side of town. We lost power, but Taj has a generator on the main house, so I ended up staying there last night."

I knew Leslie and Tamera were too shaken up by the damage to the shop when they didn't even exchange funny glances about Taj and me. They asked every other day when I was going to make a move on that man, and every other day, I said I had no plans on doing so.

Now that I had made a move, they weren't even interested.

KC, who had been on the phone, slid a device into his pocket. "Dad's on a flight out of Austin as soon as mom's nurse gets to the house."

"I can't even believe this," muttered Leslie, turning away

from the building as I had. One could only stare at the mess for so long.

"Do you need help cleaning up? I'll run home and change." I was in a terrific mood, ready to dish about my evening, so I'd dressed extra cute, in an open bust cropped hoodie, a white tank, high waisted black leggings, and converse sneakers.

"No, no," said KC, shaking his head. A heavy hand landed on my shoulder; he gave me a comforting squeeze. "The insurance company said not to touch anything until they can get out here and assess the damage, take some pictures. My dad's a general contractor. I want him to see it like this so he can let me know what it's going to take to put it back up."

"If I even put it back up," said Leslie.

"Babe," KC soothed, reaching for her. "Don't talk that way."

"Maybe it's time. Curl & Dye has been here for sixty years. Maybe this is the Universe saying it's time to let it go."

She shook off his hand and stalked across the parking lot toward KC's Escalade. We watched her hop inside, slam the door, and then bury her face in her hands.

"She's upset," said Leslie's dad.

"Yep," agreed her granddad. "Her Grandy put this place up many moons ago." He grimaced, squinting into the bright sunlight. "Be a shame to lose it, but it's not like Grandy would even know."

"Leslie would know," said KC. "As hard as she fought to keep this place open, I think we all owe it to her to make sure it goes back up. I hate to throw money around, especially when people are struggling, but…"

He glanced over his shoulder at the image of Leslie in the truck, now staring listlessly out of the windshield. "I can't think of a better place to invest it. This place is a part of my family now, too. Let's all do what we can to make sure Curl & Dye reopens."

Everyone, including me, nodded and murmured in positive tones.

Tamera tossed her arm over my shoulder. "You may as well go on back home, Vonne. We can't even get in there until the insurance man comes, and with the way the town is looking, it'll be a while until he makes his way here. We've got to see what's damaged, replace windows, all of that. I know it's hard to think about being out of work for a little bit, but we're going to try to open as soon as we can, even if it means working out of Guys N' Dolls for a little bit."

"Don't rush on account of me. I'm going to be fine. Besides," I leaned in to mutter the last part in her ear. "My landlord is suddenly rather fond of me, as of last night."

Tamera crooned a low *ooooohhh* before bumping me with her hip. "We need an update in the worst way. I'll call you later for all of the details. And I do mean *all* of them."

"You know ladies don't kiss and tell—"

"We do fuck and tell, though. So be ready to tell, because I can see the *fuck* all over your face." She nudged me in the direction of my car with a salacious grin. "Go on home. Or... *wherever*. I'll call you and let you know when we're back, but it may not be for a few days."

sixteen

. . .

TAJ

"Thanks for stopping by, Rocky."

I followed a portly gentleman in navy blue coveralls out of the front door and stood on the porch with him. He held a clipboard in one hand and a pen in the other, making a dramatic show of checking my address off on his list.

"The generator should hold out for me, but the tenant in my guest house is without power. We need that transformer."

"We're doing all we can do at the moment. There's a lot of damage around town, especially on the old side of Potter Lake. We measure everything on a one to five scale, with one being the issues that get resolved first. The transformer is a one, but we've got to check the rest of the city."

"Understood. Just keep us posted."

"Mayor Cavanaugh had his tech guy set up an alert system on the city hall website. If you log on there, the latest updates should be available. You can even get a text on your phone if you want."

I held a hand out and gave him a few strong pumps, then

watched him hop down the steps and head to the house next door.

It had been a busy morning already. The neighborhood watch had come by right after Evonne left for work to check on the house, see how we fared through last night's storm and the city-wide outage. I assured them that we were okay and sent them away with a container of Drunken Donuts each.

I'd been on the phone with Cash trying to firm up the weekend when Rocky from Potter Lake Power showed up to tell me that it would be a few days before the transformer would be replaced and the lines would be back up. That news put me in a bind.

I had planned to attend Ms. Doris' retirement ceremony and to see my family, but I'd also agreed to meet up with Guys Next Door while they were all at home.

Days without power to the guest house threatened to throw a wrench in those plans. I'd feel terrible about leaving Evonne alone. She was a grown-ass woman who could handle herself, but she'd need hot water and heat and a place to put food where it wouldn't spoil.

Meaning that I'd have to leave her at my house. Alone.

And just like I didn't like leaving her down in the guest house while I had heat and lights, I didn't like leaving her behind while the town was a mess and she was displaced. I hadn't known Evonne very long at all, maybe a couple of months, but it occurred to me that I would never have been concerned about Jaslene in a power outage. She had one of the brand new apartments downtown that I was sure were reinforced brick and could withstand a severe storm.

I was surprised to hear the garage door rolling open so early in the day. I stepped to the kitchen door and peeked down into the garage to see Evonne pulling into her spot. She cut the engine and got out. The downturn of her mouth told me something was wrong.

Instead of coming upstairs, she headed toward the other door to the guest house.

"Evonne!"

She froze and slowly turned. "Yeah."

"There's still no power down there. It's gonna be a while before they get it back on. I guess the rest of town is pretty bad—"

Evonne glanced up at me, and my mouth shut with a snap. Her eyes were glassy, and her face was wet from already shed tears.

"Hey. Are you okay?"

"I'm… I need to grab something from my place. I'll be up in a minute."

She turned on a heel and marched through the garage door. A few seconds later, I heard the door slam.

I went down the stairs and through the garage, following her path to the house. I knocked and got no answer. I knocked again and was met with silence.

"Evonne! The house doesn't have power, which means it's not safe to be there. Which means I can enter to inspect the place and the conditions if I need to. Evonne—"

I tried the knob. It was unlocked. I turned it and pushed the door open, standing on the still waterlogged rug.

"Evonne?" I heard sounds of sniffling and thumping and a bag rustling. "I'm coming in. Okay?"

More sniffling, but no one screamed at me to not come in, so I stepped inside. The house was hot, the air stuffed with stale smells. I turned the corner into the kitchen to find Evonne on her knees in front of the refrigerator dumping its entire contents into a garbage bag. I leaned against the wall, watching a very determined woman trying to do something unnecessary.

"All this stuff…" She sniffed, then coughed, then went back to dumping items in the bag. "All this stuff is going bad."

"Now it's going to stink up the garage while it sits there until garbage day. If they even pick up the garbage on Friday."

Evonne stopped moving, sitting back on her heels. Finally, a small squeak escaped. Her shoulders lurched with her quiet sobs. I let it pass without bothering her, and when she was calm again, she got up off of the floor and slammed the refrigerator door shut.

"I guess that was dumb. I needed something to take my mind off of..." She didn't finish her sentence. Instead, she pushed out a ragged breath and tugged at the tank top she wore. It had rolled up a little, showing off a wink of skin.

"Off of?" I prodded, asking quietly.

"The salon was destroyed in the storm. Windows were broken, the roof is gone, and water and dirt are everywhere. It's going to be a while before they reopen. *If* they even reopen."

"What do you mean, *if?* They're Potter Lake history, I thought."

"They are." She reached for a roll of paper towels, ripped one off and dabbed under her nose. "Leslie is saying she might let it go. KC says he doesn't care how much money it takes, it's going back up, but Leslie owns it. She could still decide not to..."

She swallowed hard, so loud that I heard it, watched her throat work through her attempt to not start crying again. "And then I'll be out of a job, and I just moved out here, and I told my parents that I had this under control and here I am, failing again and I... and I—"

Evonne's face broke into a million pieces. I stepped into the kitchen to wrap my arms around her waist before she could sink to the floor. Instead, she slumped against me, forehead against my chest until her sobbing turned to deep breaths.

When her head tipped up again, she seemed shy. A little

embarrassed, even. I didn't know Evonne to be shy or timid. I didn't want to laugh, but a chuckle slipped out. She laughed, silently at first until loud giggles erupted from her. "What the hell was that? I don't think I have ever done that."

"What? Broke down?"

"Yeah. Not...not ever."

"So it was probably overdue, then."

She moved backward, out of the safe circle of my arms. Reluctantly I let them drop.

"Can we agree on some things?" I asked. She rolled her eyes, planted a hand on her hip, and tilted her head at me. I took that as yes. "First, I don't rent this place out because I need the money." She nodded. I continued. "While I would appreciate the rent as long as you can pay it because it's not much, the place is available for as long or as short as you need it."

She inhaled a breath, ready to argue, I could feel it. I silenced her with my thumb and kept going. "And if you have to move on, let me know, even if the lease isn't up yet. I'm easy."

She bobbed her head to remove my thumb from her lips. Then said, "Don't tell women that you're easy, Nurse Dude. They'll take advantage of you."

I lifted my shoulders in a shrug, then reached around her to grab the garbage bag stuffed with food. "Whatever it is you need from down here, grab it. It's hot, and I want to get back to conditioned air, and away from whatever it is I'm smelling."

"Thai Bistro. It was already on the edge of needing to be tossed out."

I hefted the bag and headed toward the door. "I'll be at home. Don't hang out here too long. It's not safe without power."

"I don't need anything," she said, picking up the keys and

bag she'd dropped when she came in. "I came down here to cry by myself."

"Oh. I ruined that, looks like." I walked out, then waited for her to pull the door shut and lock it.

A few minutes later, we were back in the cool, good smelling house, settled in chairs at the kitchen island. The sun was doing its job, bringing natural light into the room. The residual scent of the pulled pork sandwiches I'd made for lunch lingered in the air. It was early in the day, but it had already been eventful, so I didn't know about Evonne, but I needed a little nip.

I cracked open the whiskey and a can of Coke and poured us both a drink.

"Breakdown notwithstanding," she said, her fingers trembling as they circled the rim of the glass, "I'll be okay. I have savings, and there are other shops where I could work. I have to keep the faith that Leslie will reopen. Like KC said, she fought too hard to let it close. Besides, we aren't the same failing shop anymore. We *have* to reopen."

"I can't believe they would even think not to."

"Me either. And not only because I like The Curl & Dye. I like that people trust me enough to sit in my chair and say, 'give me something that looks good' and I do what I think looks good and they love it. I can do that anywhere, but I want to do that for the same people I've been doing that for."

"Like you said, keep the faith. But for now, the shop is closed for a little bit, huh?"

"Yup. Forced vacation." She tipped a swallow from the glass into her mouth. "I've never had whiskey before."

"I'm corrupting you, Miss Girard?"

"Not hardly, Nurse Dude. Me and Eb sneak a little of my Daddy's bourbon now and then. He keeps it for special occasions. And Edison, if we go to visit him, likes gin and vodka and scotch. Just no whiskey."

"My dad turned me on to it. He and my grandfather drink whiskey. What do you think?"

"Sets my throat on fire, and then what's left is like… a spiced vanilla flavor." She swirled the glass in a circular motion, watching the liquor splash up on the sides. "I can't describe it. I could get used to it."

"There's plenty where that came from. Help yourself."

"Don't mind if I do," she said, picking up the bottle of Crown Royal Vanilla and pouring a couple of splashes into her glass. "You've been very accommodating, Nurse Dude. You didn't have to open up your house to me. Serve your top shelf alcohol and your boozy donuts and put me up in a room in the ivory tower. I appreciate it."

"You're one of those weepy, feeling drunks." I tipped my glass back, finishing the last swallow. "Are you tipsy at one in the afternoon?"

"I've had a rough day!" She protested, her voice sounding grittier than usual, either from the emotional bout or alcohol. Whatever caused it, it was sexy. "Well, we heard about how my job is going. How's the clinic?"

I shrugged. "I guess it's still standing. I don't have to darken those doors until next week, so I don't care."

"Next week? I thought nurses worked a lot."

"I do!" I screeched, almost offended. "I work three twelve-hour shifts a week unless I pick up overtime. Which I do, because what else am I supposed to do with my time?"

"Go out? Have fun? Play a sport? Watch a sport? Do anything but work?"

I shrugged. "I'm not into that, I guess. I'm new here. I don't have people to do that with."

"You've been here long enough to buy a house, renovate it and get a tenant. You're not new anymore."

Evonne rolled her eyes and sipped more of her drink. "Don't worry about that, though. I'll introduce you around. You should at least hang with the guys at the barbershop.

Erik and KC and Kendrick and those guys? You'd have fun with them."

"I'm not a *hang out at the barbershop* kind of guy."

"They do more than that. They work together, is all."

She'd started to tip the glass back and let the last swallow of whiskey slide down her throat, but stopped, dropping it back to the countertop with a thunk.

"Hey, since we're both off for a little bit, we should go out! There's a couple of cool new restaurants, or the new Cineplex, or the Kit Kat Lounge, which is okay, I guess—"

"Actually, Evonne, I had another idea in mind. I had plans to head down to Jacksonville this weekend. There's an event I need to attend but I mostly want to see my friends and family— "

"Oh. Well…" Her expression changed; her eyes darted around the room. "We can hang out another time when you're back. Maybe the next time you have a day off…"

"No, no," I interrupted, waving my hands around. "Thing is, I don't want to leave you here by yourself this weekend when the town is a mess, and there's no power. The generator will hold up, but who knows if the grocery store will be open, you know? You're off anyway, so I was thinking… well, why don't you come with me? We could have a chill couple of days on the Florida coast, and it'll give the city time to get back on its feet."

It was like I hadn't said anything to her at all. She stared at me, her face a blank slate.

"Evonne? What do you think?"

seventeen

. . .

EVONNE

What do I think? Is he serious? What do I think?

Taj's lips moved, but my ears stopped processing sound at the words *why don't you come with me.*

This man that I had only known enough to say hello and joke around with...and have sex with wanted me to get into a car and leave city limits with him. We hadn't so much as been on a date but he wanted me to travel with him. To another state?

He'd started talking again, but I interrupted his spiel with a hand to his chest. I closed my eyes and sucked in a breath, then opened them again, prepared to barrel forward in telling him he was nuts if he thought I would agree to travel alone with him.

The excitement in his eyes, the hope in his face at the prospect of a road trip, stopped me cold.

"Taj, I—"

"I know. You're concerned about your safety. I could be dangerous. I could be a serial killer."

"That's so comforting, considering you live next door."

"And you listen to an almost constant barrage of murder stories. You'd be crazy to consider it."

"And yet you're asking me to."

"I'll cover everything: transportation, food, housing, fun… *everything*. You don't have to spend a thin dime. If you want to send my information to Ebony so she can make sure you're okay, that's cool with me. Whatever would make you feel safe."

On the one hand: It would be nice to get out of town for a few days. Relax, do some sightseeing. Let someone take care of me for once.

On the other hand: This wasn't a good idea.

On the other *other* hand: Neither was fucking my landlord, and that worked out okay.

If the town was going to be without power for days, my only other option was to drive to Healy and spend a few days at my parent's house. That would not be a good idea.

Taj leaned in and kissed me as if proximity and soft lips would break down the last barrier. "If it sweetens the pot," he said quietly, "I talked my mom into making her sausage lasagna and garlic bread. It's the best I've ever tasted, and you don't want to miss it."

My mouth watered at the mention of hearty pasta, red sauce, and fresh crusty, buttery garlic bread. That would hit the spot after days of takeout and four hours in the car. "I *am* a greedy bitch that loves food."

"The weather will damn sure be nicer than it is here. And, you know, full power. No downed trees, no electrical lines on the ground. Do any of your podcasts talk about people being electrocuted?"

"Okay, all right." I tossed up my hands in defeat. Then I admitted to myself that I'd decided I wanted to go as soon as he suggested it, but I had to talk myself into it. "But if we're leaving today, I need to go back to my place and *pack*, pack."

Taj rolled his eyes at my declaration. "How long does it take to *pack*, pack?"

"Should be no big thing," I said, getting up from the island, but not before downing the last of the whiskey and Coke in my glass. I laughed at his audible groan, setting my glass next to his. "Be ready in a few."

"Minutes?" He asked, his expression naively hopeful.

"Oh, baby…" I dropped a kiss on his cheek before heading to the staircase. "Hours."

———

"Mama's gonna *lose. her. mind*, Vonnie!"

I adjusted my earbuds because Ebony's shriek was excruciating. I had to call her at work to share my newly developed weekend plans, not only because I would be out of town, but because in the span of a day, my relationship with Taj had seen major changes.

Sort of. We weren't anything official. *Friendly*. But open with our attraction to each other. I would have a good time getting to know him, and this weekend would give me a master's class in Taj Wright.

And who knew what could happen after that?

"First of all," I told her, going back to packing my suitcase. "I'm grown. I'm not concerned with what Mama is gonna think."

"Oh, now that she's all moved out, she don't care what Mama thinks."

"That's right! If she could kick me out at any minute, I'd be concerned about her approval, but I don't live under her roof anymore, so I don't care. Still…"

I tossed a couple of pairs of my favorite leggings, the ones with the pockets that I saw all over Instagram, into my suitcase. Along with those, a few new tops that were cute but classy enough to wear around his family. I rounded out the selection with a few sundresses and a long, comfortable maxi dress to ride in.

"Don't you say anything to her. All she needs to know is that I'm fine. Daddy, either. Not Edison, not the boys and definitely not Grandma Bobbie. The entire east coast will know before dinner if you tell her."

I sometimes wished my parents would move Grandma Bobbie to Primrose Gardens, Potter Lake's Assisted Living facility. I could visit her more often, and she'd be the delight of this little town. I never met a woman that gossiped more than Grandma Bobbie.

Maybe my next goal should be to rescue her from Mama.

"I'll keep your raggedy little secret. You're really doing the landlord, huh?"

"You say that like it's one of those romance books you read. You know, like *The Truck Driver's Secret Affair*."

Ebony cackled. "More like *The Billionaire's Cute Girlfriend That He Randomly Met at Kroger*. Let's manifest some love in this bitch!"

I cackled aloud and went back to packing.

"Answer my question, Vonne! Is he any good?"

My skin flushed at flashes from the night before: wrestling around with Taj, the glisten of sweat on our skin, the heavy breaths, the desperate clinging, the satisfying scratch of an itch.

"I'm *doing the landlord*, as you put it," I responded. "Yeah. And yes, he's good. Really good. Up all night, good."

She clicked her tongue, and I'm sure I heard eyes roll. "You make me sick. You know I was about to make my move."

"Where? When? Every time you come out here, he's at work."

"I was going to! At some point!"

"Eb, be happy for me. This is like that episode of *Black*

Women's Mental Health, on When Your Friends Can't Clap for You. Clap for me, bitch."

I snorted, then, because all I could hear was Ebony's ferocious clapping into the mic.

In my years of adulting, few as they were, I'd never dated a man that took me on a trip. Not even my college fling.

I hadn't thought about him in a long, *long* time. I was surprised Taj got me to talk about him, but alcohol was involved. Drunk was the only way I would acknowledge Terrell Hawkins. When I ran headlong into trouble, and he disappeared, melted away like butter on a hotcake, I'd put him out of my mind. I hardly ever called him by name. I didn't like giving him that much power.

When he began popping up everywhere with that music group, I made a point to ignore him and them. I couldn't fall for the *guy next door*, friendly dude vibe they tried to push to the public. The others were probably the same— dogs traveled in packs.

Taj was older than the men I'd dated before, held a steady job, had an advanced degree, owned a home, and rented out part of it to me. In short, Taj was a grown-ass man. I'd never had one of those before.

So it was a quick trip he'd already planned.

So he asked me along, mainly out of pity and not wanting to leave me in his home by myself. I took it as a good omen, and I planned to see this trip for what it was, straight on: a chance to get the hell out of town with a man I wanted to get the hell out of town with.

"I'm packed, at least from my stuff down here," I told Ebony after I'd tossed a few pairs of shoes into the almost full suitcase yawning open on the bed. "I need to go back to the house, pack my shower stuff—"

"I don't need a play by play of your getaway with fine ass Nurse Dude. Call me when you get to town. And call me if you have any issues. And call me to let me know how things are going."

"So… call you?"

"Call meeeee," she whined, then giggled and hung up. I popped out my earbuds, grabbed my suitcase, and rolled it out of the house.

An hour later, I was the one standing at the door with a suitcase and my backpack, playing Words with Friends with Grandma Bobbie. When Taj finally made it downstairs, lugging a slim and sturdy Samsonite, I tried my best to stifle a bubble of laughter but was unsuccessful.

"Sorry," he said, panting and ignoring my giddiness at beating him downstairs. "Are you ready?"

"Don't even, Nurse Dude. I've been standing here forever. Let's go. I can taste the lasagna already."

eighteen

. . .

TAJ

The elephant in the room— actually lodged in my throat, was choking me.

I knew I'd have to come clean about Guys Next Door at some point before we walked into a room, and they were all sitting there. I'd had so many chances to tell Evonne about a massive part of my life and let all of them slip past me. I'd had the entire drive to open up and tell her and still hadn't.

I could say that I didn't know why I hadn't told her, but I did. I didn't want anything to change between us.

I preferred to keep them under wraps, to introduce them to people and my association with them on my terms, so there were no photos of the guys on my walls, no gold records, no Lucite awards casually displayed in the bookcases. When I'd been able to attend a show, I never took pictures with them, and they respected my wishes to not appear on their social media pages.

We had a chat app that we used when needed. I knew

their addresses, their phone numbers, their middle names. I knew those guys in real life and that life was sacred.

It was also *my* past and not something that I wanted to be hoisted on my shoulders to carry around for the rest of my life.

Cash's proposition weeks earlier to rejoin The Guys Next Door rolled around and around in my head. I went back and forth on my decision, trying to find a way that I could make it work, then deciding that it would be too difficult and would draw too much attention. My life would never be normal again, and a long, healthy life was what I craved.

In Potter Lake, I was Taj Wright. Not even cancer survivor Taj Wright; not many people knew that part of my past, either. I had a completely different life there. I couldn't be gone from my regular job for months at a time for recording, rehearsing and touring.

My eyes drifted from the road to the woman in the passenger seat of my car in a heather grey t-shirt dress and sandals. Whatever she'd used on her short cut with bouncy curls up top smelled like almonds. I'd expected her face to be buried in her phone during the entire drive, but she was alert, asking questions, making jokes, genuinely interested in the changing landscape from dusty Georgia to lush, green Florida.

Though I'd practically begged her to, I was surprised that she'd agreed to come on this trip; now that we were almost to our destination, I was nervous about what she was going to find out. The decision that I was sure I'd be forced to make would mean choosing to leave a woman I'd started something with, however casual, to hop on stages all over the world and sing songs to other women. None of the guys had managed to make a relationship work and still be a part of the group. I didn't want to fall prey to that curse, too.

"I've never been outside of Georgia," Evonne blurted, puncturing the quiet sounds of wheels on the pavement and the low thump of a satellite radio station. I'd asked to listen to music for a change of pace after two hours of podcasts.

"Never? Not in your whole life?"

Evonne shook her head. "Furthest I ever went was Atlanta. That was my big chance. I was supposed to graduate and stay in the big city and get a high paying job. Like Edison."

She uttered a sarcastic, "*Tuh*. I couldn't even do that right. Ended up right back in little ol' Healy. Doing press and curls at a sixty-year-old salon."

I reached over to her, feeling for the hand I knew was curled inside the other on her lap. I wound my fingers between hers and brought our hands to my lap. I squeezed her hand in mine, then stole another glance at her.

"Maybe the shop will get a little facelift. A little push into the future."

"I wish I would have seen what my life would turn out to be. I wish I hadn't gone to that party and made a fool of myself. I wish I hadn't been so naive, so stupid with—"

"You should wish," I interrupted with another squeeze to her hand, "to be able to let go of the past. What's done is done. Atlanta is back there in the rearview mirror. Don't look back; it distracts from the now. You're right where you need to be, Evonne."

Her exhale seemed to come from the depths of her soul. She sat back, balancing her head against the cushioned head-rest. "Can you see the ocean from Jacksonville?"

"Jax proper? No. But the house is only about a half-hour from Jacksonville Beach."

She gave a low wolf whistle while staring out of the wind-shield. "So close. You were probably at the beach every week-end, huh?"

"Mmmmm…" I mused, tipping my head side to side. "You know that saying, you don't know what you've got until it's gone? I didn't realize how rarely we went to the beach until I wasn't close to it anymore. Even when I come home, I forget. You want to go?"

Her head whipped around so fast I thought it might fly off her neck. She grinned, her whole face aglow. "Really? Won't it put us out of the way? I'd love to see it. Just drive by."

"We can do more than drive by Evonne."

It was cute the way she squeezed her fingers, still wrapped up in mine. She slapped her thigh with her other hand and exclaimed, "The ocean!" with a sigh.

Making Evonne make that sound, and other sounds, meant she was happy. Making her happy, I realized, was something I wanted to keep doing.

nineteen

. . .

EVONNE

Ocean water is warm.

I stood holding fists of my dress bunched up around my thighs while the tide rushed over my feet, up to my knees, and out again. I could have stood there, a few feet out from the shoreline, for hours.

"I can't believe I've never seen the ocean! I feel so small."

"Small?" he repeated from behind me.

Taj had pulled a blanket from the trunk and spread it out on the hot sand. He didn't want to get his feet wet, and he hated sand between his toes. I managed to talk him into taking his shoes off and wading into the water for a few minutes, though. When I was sufficiently mesmerized by the rhythmic flow of waves, he quietly escaped to the blanket so his feet could dry.

"The vastness of the ocean... like, there's nothing in the distance. It's so huge. I feel like I'm standing on a tiny piece of the planet right here. It's overwhelming."

"I guess I can see that. I feel like that sometimes."

I turned to find him leaning back on his palms; his legs stretched out so that his feet received maximum sun. I walked back to the blanket and sat down beside him.

"Done playing in the ocean already?" he asked, leaning in my direction. I met him halfway and pressed my lips to his.

"Guess I'll dry off, too," I said, mimicking his pose.

"We have plenty of time, Evonne. I'm not rushing you. It's peaceful out here."

"Will this be our only trip to the beach?"

"Hope not."

"Well, then. We have lasagna to eat." We laughed together. Then sighed, together. Then laughed again. "What do you have to feel overwhelmed about?" I asked.

He huffed a laugh, looking away. "Lots of things. My life is nice—"

"*Really* nice."

"But nice things don't make it perfect. The cancer is always in the back of my mind. Logically, I know that I can't control recurrence. All I can do is live my life. I've been cancer-free for a long time, but what if?"

"Yeah. I've been thinking about it since you told me, and it's only been a day."

"Right. And there's the work I do. Do I want to stay where I am, where the work isn't all that challenging? Or keep climbing the ladder, maybe go for a Master's in Nursing? Maybe get a job in a particular field—"

"Like Oncology?"

He didn't confirm that. But didn't deny it, either. He sat up, bringing his knees up and resting his elbows on them.

"One of the reasons I'm home this weekend is to drop by this retirement party for one of the nurses I had when I was sick. She was a battle ax. But I liked her because she didn't treat me with kid gloves. She wasn't afraid to be tough—she'd seen the worst. She told the truth. But she also told me to fight. So I fought."

"Nursing isn't a thing a guy typically wants to do with his life. Why not a doctor or a nurse practitioner?"

"Because it's not the same. Not to me. There's a level of care, the level that I got, I want to give back. In the same way. But…" He sighed, his gaze moving from the ocean waves to my questioning eyes. "I've been holding off on a lot of things, and I don't know if now is the time to move. I have so many choices I could make. I can't make any of them. I don't know which way to go. I'm paralyzed by the options."

I sensed that he was hinting at something more profound. And that he wasn't ready to open up about it. But also that he wanted to. But maybe not with his tenant, that he happened to be sleeping with because it was fun.

"I know one thing, though." He turned so he could stand, then offered a hand to me. "There's a giant pan of lasagna and garlic bread at the house. My brothers love free food and will eat it all if we don't get there."

I let him pull me up, then grabbed up the blanket, shook it out, and folded it. Taj carried both pairs of shoes, and we picked our way through the sand to the car. In minutes, we were back on the highway.

———

The Wright family home was as lovely as I imagined it would be. Simple from the outside, but from the lush green lawn to the manicured trees and bushes, the brick front home was well cared for. Taj turned into the driveway and parked next to a car already sitting in front of the garage. A sleek two-door coupe was parked at the curb.

He pressed the ignition button to kill the engine but didn't get out of the car.

"Listen, before we go in, I want you to know there's no pressure. My family knows you're coming with me. They're cool with it. They know you're my tenant. They know we're... *friendly*."

My eyebrows shot up into my hairline. "You told your family we're fucking?"

Taj laughed. "Not in so many words. The more open I am with them, the less they pry, so yes. I was frank with them. I like you, and they know that. Mostly, I don't want my mom asking about grandchildren and calling you her daughter in law already. But don't worry," he said, that mischievous grin I knew well popping out. "I didn't tell them about that tongue swirl thing you do when you—"

"Okay, okay... we don't have to rehash it. Right now."

Taj paused, his focus moving from me to something beyond me. Then his face lit up at the sight of the front door swinging open. A middle-aged couple stepped out onto the porch, then waved from the top step, both smiling like crazy.

"Aw, they're so happy to see you!" For some reason, I was surprised by this. "They're so cute!"

He popped the door latch and hopped out, then hurried around to my side. "Ready for this?" he asked, offering a hand to help me out.

I slung my bag over one shoulder and took the offered hand. He didn't let go as he shut the door behind me, and we crossed the driveway together.

His parents met us halfway, grinning ear to ear. Taj was a replica of his father in every way but his height, from the dark tone of his skin to the light brown hue of his eyes. They had the same facial structure, spoke in the same tenor, had the same moderately stocky build.

"Randall," he said, gripping my hand gently. "This is my wife, Theresa."

Taj's mother was a bitty thing, shorter than I was with a runner's physique. She came at me, beaming, and hugged me with the strength of a bodybuilder.

"Evonne!" She exclaimed when she had released me. "It is

so great to meet you! Taj talks about you all the time. I'm so excited that you're here!"

"All the time, you say?"

"Ma! We talked about this—"

She looped her arm around my elbow and began guiding us into the house. "Oh, yes, he told us all about the salon where you work, said it's the most popular one in town, so you must know what you're doing. He also said you know a lot about skincare and hair products, and I have some questions for you..." She prattled on and on about morning routines and products she was using.

I peered over my shoulder at Taj, who was in pace behind us, trying hard to hide his smirk.

My stomach growled loudly as soon as I stepped into the house, the scent of pasta and sauce and cheese and garlic filling the air overwhelmed me in the most delicious way.

"Is Squirt here?" A booming voice thundered from somewhere in the house. "I'm getting *hangry,* and I'm tired of eating bread!"

I giggled, and then my breath caught in my throat. Two wide chested, broad-shouldered, taller-than- your average tall black men lumbered around the corner.

"Sup," said one of them, nodding to me. His neat locs fell forward as he bent to offer me an enormous hand. "I'm Kyle. That's Brandon," he explained, angling a thumb at the other. "Welcome."

"Hi. Thanks. Sorry to hold up dinner."

"Honey, you didn't hold up a thing. They're always hungry. That's why we had to kick them out." Theresa led the group to the dining room, where a large table stood ready for dinner. Randall took his place at the head of the table.

"Can I help with anything?" I asked.

"No, no. We're ready to eat. I was keeping the lasagna warm in the oven. Boys, one of you grab the salad and dressing and bring it to the table. And did you leave any bread for the rest of us?"

"Yes ma'am," came the deep but monotone reply, in unison. On the way to the kitchen, they stopped to wrap meaty arms around Taj, putting him in a headlock, rubbing the top of his head, and calling him Squirt.

"Get off me, meatheads," I heard him protest through pants and laughter. "I'm still the oldest, with your overgrown asses."

"Oldest doesn't count when we can stomp you, Squirt."

"Ma would never let you stomp me."

"Stop that nonsense and sit so that we can eat." Theresa directed me to sit, then ordered Taj to take the spot next to me.

"You said your brothers were both bigger than you," I muttered to Taj. "You didn't say they were giants."

"They're friendly giants."

"They were kind of puny until about...what, junior year of high school?" Randall stared off to his right, accessing his memories. "Anyway, they shot up after that. My side of the family has height, but none of us are built like these boys."

"I'm the normal one," Taj boasted, grabbing my plate. He dished up a healthy serving of lasagna, added some green salad alongside, and a few slices of garlic bread before setting it back down in front of me.

"Normal is a relative term," said Brandon.

"He's about to launch into that tired Ted Talk he's been obsessed with for the last six months," said Kyle, his hands poised over a full plate. "Evonne, what do you get into? And how do you like renting from Squirt?"

"I have a name..." Taj protested, around a mouthful. "Why does no one know my name?"

The family hadn't heard how Taj and I met— not the full story anyway, so I shared, replete with all of the overblown drama and his refusal to take me seriously. They ribbed him, and rightly so, for his reaction. He shrugged in response, cleaning his plate and going for a second helping.

"I'm into art, more modern, but I can appreciate art history. At Spelman…"

I cut myself off before I even went down that path. I'd aced Art History, but there would surely be questions about my experience at an HBCU, and not everyone needed to know I was a college dropout.

"Anyway, I like movies and music, like most people. My sister and I have listened to every podcast in existence. But I spend most of my time researching and running my website. I give reviews and skin tips for men and women. I take a lot of webinars on the science of skincare and—"

I paused, laughing, and blushing on the inside. "Y'all don't care about that…"

"I do," Brandon said. "I work for the FDA. We have limited authority over cosmetics and beauty products, but yeah, getting these junk science products outta here? Right up my alley."

"That's probably why this one has such great skin." I stroked Taj's cheek; he leaned into my palm, giving it a greasy kiss.

"Naw, Squirt don't listen to me. He's just lucky."

Dinner conversation bounced from Randall's talk about his work at the local paper processing plant, Theresa's upcoming summer break from her job teaching third graders, and Kyle's new role as one of the coaches for the Jacksonville State football team.

I thoroughly enjoyed myself, feeling looped into every conversation. When the boys were full—which took some time— and the meal appeared to be over, I picked up my plate and Taj's and headed to the kitchen where Theresa was loading the dishwasher.

"Thank you, sweetheart. Could you grab the lasagna pan and the salad bowl for me?"

"Sure," I said, happy to be able to help, and turned around to head back to the dining room.

"What do you mean, she doesn't know yet?" I heard Brandon ask. I froze, then dove around the corner. "How long do you think you can keep it from her?"

"I mean, we're down here," Taj replied. "I'm supposed to see them, so not much longer."

"You should have already told her," said Brandon.

"You know I don't like to talk about that with people. I like for a woman to like me for me—"

"Come on with that *like me for me* bullshit," Kyle argued. "That's weak sauce. You want somebody to fall in love with poor Taj so you can drop the bomb on 'em."

"I'm not trying to drop anything on Evonne. I want to take my time. I will tell her. Soon. But you can't blame me; you know how women get when they find out—"

"Find out what?"

"Evonne." Taj seemed to jump out of his skin when I swept into the room, a hand on one hip. "Shit."

"I didn't mean to eavesdrop, but I heard all of that. And I heard my name, so there's something I need to know. Taj?"

"No choice now, Squirt," said Brandon, shoving the last piece of garlic bread into his mouth.

Taj leveled a glare at his brothers, his top lip curled in a way I'd never seen before. "I... guess I need to show you something."

He pushed his chair back, then nodded his head for me to follow him. We walked through the house to a door, then took steps to the basement.

"This isn't your dungeon where you tie up women and leave them for dead, is it?"

"Sure, with my family right upstairs. You listen to too many podcasts, Evonne."

The basement was finished, decked out with the most beautiful home theater I'd ever seen. "Whoa," I breathed, slowing as I passed the large screen television, oversized couches and chairs, even a popcorn machine and a well-stocked cooler.

"Where do you think the idea for my living room came from? My dad is big into movies; he wanted a place to watch them in the comfort of his own home. We built out this spot a few years ago. Come this way," he said, walking through the room and down a hallway to a closed door.

"Another sanctuary?" I guessed.

"Kind of." He turned the knob and reached to flip on the overhead light. He let me enter, following close behind into a room that was rather dull— standard-issue curtains on the windows, bland carpeting, construction beige wall paint— except for the items that had been stuffed inside of it.

Along one wall were plaques, small ones, and large ones, some bearing gold and silver records. A glass cabinet lined another wall with framed photos and... *Grammy* awards?

"What is this room, Taj?" I stepped closer, reading some of the plaques. Song of the Year. Album of the Year. Video Single. Boxed Set Sales.

"This is the other part of my life. The part I haven't told you about."

Taj pointed to one of the photos. I stepped forward, studying one of him with four familiar faces. The photo was years old; Taj was much younger; his face was noticeably rounded, swollen from chemotherapy treatments.

My throat closed up, and I wanted to vomit every bite I'd eaten.

He was young in the photo, but I could pick him out anywhere; the man that I'd met at Spelman, who'd dated me, then tossed me aside for someone else— younger, older, more experienced, less naive— it didn't matter. He'd stranded me at a party I had no business attending, who had left me to fend for myself in the aftermath.

"Guys Next Door." I turned to face him, my arms folded tightly across my chest. "You're saying that you know them?"

"They're my friends. Closer than friends, practically family. We grew up together in this neighborhood. We started the group together. We landed a deal together. And then I got sick, and I couldn't tour, so they got this other guy—"

If I'd never met him, I'd have never been suspended. I'd have never ended up back at home. I'd have never been a disappointment to Rhonda Girard. Every wrong thing that had happened to me since that night happened because of him.

"Terrell Hawkins," I whispered.

twenty

. . .

TAJ

"Yeah. Terrell."

I reached out to pick up the photo, using the hem of my t-shirt to wipe non-existent dust off of the frame and glass. My mother did a great job of keeping the room clean and up to date.

"He replaced you, then. All of his parts in their songs are supposed to be yours. So, how is he? I mean, does he sound like you?"

"He does all right. I guess I hear it how I would sing it."

Evonne was quieter, calmer, and less enamored than I expected her to be. The Guys Next Door would have been popular during her college years— they'd been topping the charts by then. The fans, which the group lovingly called *Neighbors,* were rabid, obsessed, and dedicated.

"You weren't a Neighbor, then? A Guys Next Door fan?"

"What makes you ask?"

I set the photo back in its spot in the case and stepped back. "You seem… unimpressed."

"I'm not fangirling because you know famous people." I detected an eye roll before she turned toward the wall, where all of the awards that the group had won were hung. "Why do you have these, though? The Grammys, the albums? You weren't in the group."

"Because I won them. I wrote the songs that won those awards."

The reaction that I'd been waiting for was, at that very moment, rolling across her face. I watched her eyes grow with the realization of what this room meant to me, what my hidden dreams, goals, and accomplishments were about and what I was trying to share with her.

"All of these..." Her brows rose. Her mouth dropped open. "These are all for songs you wrote?"

"Only the singles that sold enough to win an award. Gold, platinum, multi-platinum, diamond; if I write it and it wins something, I get one too. That's how I stay connected to them. Involved in the group without singing a note."

"Taj...you're fine, now. You've *been* fine. Enough to get a degree and a job. You didn't want to go back to the group?"

I lifted a shoulder in a relaxed, couldn't-care-less shrug, though that was far from the case. "It would have been noticeable to switch Terrell out. I didn't want to cause drama, make it harder on the other guys. Also, Terrell had a contract. I couldn't take his gig from him if I wanted to."

Evonne took one last glance around the room, then closed the distance between us in a few steps. Her arms slid around my neck and rested on my shoulders. My arms closed around her. I moved in even closer until we were nose to nose.

"You're trying to impress me, aren't you, Nurse Dude?"

"Not really," I said, shaking my head. "I would have told you on day one, had all this stuff up at my house if I was trying to impress you."

"This is why you have a piano." I nodded. "And you don't regret not going back?"

I deflected, opting to flirt instead of being completely honest. "Right now? At this specific minute?" I grinned, letting my hands drop from her waist to the generous roundness of her behind. Then I moved lower to her thigh and lifted her leg, so it wrapped around my body. "Not so much."

Evonne laughed. I felt it through her chest pressed into mine. "Taj, be serious."

"I am serious. Since you don't seem to be into the group, this is a moment that I'd never have if I'd been TDub, of the Guys Next Door."

"TDub," she repeated, her brows high again.

"TDub, the Sexy Tenor. You know what I mean?"

"Oh, I kn—*ohhhh…*" The last of her sentence trailed off as my lips made contact with her skin. Her scent was sexy, like musky jasmine. She was soft yet firm in all the right places, her body literally wrapped around mine.

I trailed the sharp line of her chin to her lips and pressed my mouth to hers. Lightly at first, then with more fervor when she responded in kind. I groaned, feeling myself come to life, thrust into her body. I clutched a handful of her thigh and pulled her into me, up against my growing erection. The roll of her hips and the low rumble that came from deep inside her lit me up. I inhaled, sucking air through my nose because I wasn't releasing her lips any time soon.

Nothing else in the room existed. We could have been in Times Square, and it wouldn't have mattered. It was Evonne and me, and the sounds of pleasured groaning, our tongues madly, passionately swirling, our bodies moving together in a sensual rhythm.

"Taj…hold…hold *on!*" Evonne broke the kiss and tried to step back, but I had her in a vice grip. "We can't disrespect your parents in their house—"

"I am a grown man—"

"In your mama's house!" She protested, laughing as she

wrenched herself out of my arms. "With your— and I can't stress this enough — *big* brothers upstairs."

"All right, okay. Can I get a raincheck on everything we were doing just now, though?"

"Boy, did you hear me say *your mama's house*?"

"Why do you think I told them we were together?"

"They probably still don't expect us to get down and dirty."

"Evonne..."

"Taj!" She giggled. "I know we aren't serious, but I'm not trying to make a bad impression on your parents. The bed might be knocking against the wall and shit."

I sucked my teeth, giving in for now.

"None of this does anything for you, huh? I wasted my time being worried about your reaction to all of this?"

"This?" Evonne waved a hand at various objects around the room. "It's cool. I like seeing all this stuff. Ebony will probably be impressed."

I shoved my hands in my pockets and paused for a few beats. Then said quietly, "It's not Ebony that I want to be impressed, Evonne."

"Taj... I get it." She soothed me with a kiss, then pulled back before we could pick up where we left off. "You keep all this stuff squirreled in a room at the back of your parent's basement. You don't want it to define you, but it is a part of you, part of your life, your history. You needed to trust me, to let me in. I'm happy you do."

"Well, I should also tell you that—"

"Taj!" Kyle was calling, his heavy steps giving him away. "You still down here, Squirt?"

I pushed out a breath, pinching the bridge of my nose. "In here, Kyle," I called back. In moments, the doorway was filled with broad shoulders. He reached above him to the frame of the door, resting his fist against the edge.

"Ma is bringing out the cobbler and ice cream. Dad is itching to play Tonk. Y'all coming'?"

"Tonk?" Evonne looked to me for an explanation.

"She don't know about Tonk, either?" Kyle laid a heavy arm across her shoulders, guiding us out of the room toward the basement steps. "Something *else* Taj hasn't told you about. It's a card game we've been playing since we were kids. Used to be for points, now it's for money."

"I'd watch if I were you," I advised from behind them. "They *will* take your money."

"I prefer to call it 'liberating people of their disposable income.' I will take Squirt's money. He's got enough of it."

"I don't know why you assume I would lose, Nurse Dude. I am vicious."

"Yeah, *Nurse Dude*…"

"As vicious as a puppy. You didn't come close to winning UNO last night."

"A hand we haven't finished *playing*. I've got my game face on. Come on here so I can kick your ass at whatever Tonk is."

twenty-one

. . .

EVONNE

I'd lost the first game, but after that won every hand. I was sure, being seasoned players, that I was getting special treat-ment and they were letting me win, but Taj's attitude at my victories told me differently. After losing twice, he threw down his cards and went to the kitchen for more cobbler.

After they'd tired of losing to me, the game folded, and the brothers stayed for a movie. Theresa and Randall went to bed in the middle of it, so Taj and I said good night to his brothers and unloaded the luggage from the car.

More cheerfully than was necessary, I bounded into the room that Taj and I would be staying in for the weekend. His parents had been considerate of the fact that we'd probably want to be alone, so they let us choose the guest bedroom downstairs at the opposite end of the house from their bedroom.

The room was a near carbon copy of Taj's bedroom in Potter Lake, only smaller. The same color scheme — blue, white and taupe, the same decor and the same arrangement, less the fireplace. Instead of a couch, there was an overstuffed chair and ottoman next to a bookcase.

"So, Tonk was fun!"

Taj trailed me, rolling both of our suitcases, my backpack slung over one shoulder.

"More for you than for me," he said, huffing with the effort to lift my suitcase onto the bed. He set my backpack down next to it and dropped his hands to his knees. He paused to suck in a dramatic breath. "We need to talk about how much packing is necessary for a weekend. That thing is heavy."

"We don't need to talk about anything, Nurse Dude." I walked around the bed and proceeded to unzip my suitcase. It was stuffed to the brim with everything I knew I needed. And more than a few things I could need over the weekend. "You're just salty that I beat you."

"No, I'm not." He reached for his suitcase and laid it on the floor, then unzipped it and flayed it open. "I'm salty that my brothers taught you all of the tricks and told you *how* to beat me."

I dug through my luggage, pulling out items for my shower, my cleansers, and utensils for my evening routine. Once they were in a pile, I zipped the suitcase closed again and set it next to the bed.

"I like your brothers. They are friendly giants."

"They were on their best behavior."

"Which one of them... you know... gave you stem cells?"

"Brandon. I'm surprised he didn't bring it up. He loves knowing that he saved my life."

I pulled my dress over my head and unhooked my bra, then tossed them on top of the suitcase. Then I sat down and reached for my brush, tea tree oil moisturizing spray, and silk scarf.

I spritzed my hair, then pulled a brush through it. "Y'all let me win, didn't you?"

When I got no response, I repositioned so I could see him. He was still on the floor in front of his suitcase, both fists planted in the piles of neatly stacked clothing.

He was staring at me, his jaw slack.

"What'd I say?"

"Noth— nothing." He blinked, then blinked again. "You … you're…"

"Ohhh." I laughed. "Titties, huh?"

His lips bent into an embarrassed, but dreamy smile. He managed to move his stare to the suitcase, concentrating hard on the muted blues of the jeans atop one stack.

"I just… was thinking about last night."

"What about last night? You're not having second thoughts, are you?"

"Nope," he answered quickly, then tipped his head up to meet my gaze. "I meant I was thinking about those titties last night. Are you? Having second thoughts?"

"Not at all." I wrapped a green scarf around my hair and tucked in the ends. "I didn't wear this last night, though. You still think I'm sexy?"

"Girl… as *fuck*."

He grabbed a leather case from under the clothing and zipped it open, pulling out a small square package. Then he stood, stepped over my suitcase, and stopped in front of me. He bent over, dropping a kiss onto my lips.

Then another, but softer, sweeter, more teasing. My lips parted, my tongue peeking out to taste him. He took that opportunity to pounce, bringing his knees up onto the bed and pushing me back.

Taj fit so naturally between my thighs that my legs wrapped around him by instinct. His mouth felt so naturally good when he sucked on my tongue, then dipped to my already taut nipples. He took them into his mouth, moaning quietly. He hunched his hips into me, pressing his hardening erection into my core. I tilted my hips in rhythm with him, giving as much as I got and then some.

"Vonne..." His breath was a husky near-whisper and warm on my skin. "I want to fuck you so bad right now."

"*Unh...*" I shuddered at the pleasant pain of pressure quickly building.

"I would come home every night and think about how close you were to me. Maybe I could kiss you again. Maybe suck on your lips, your toes, your ears. Maybe suck on everything you got, that I can suck on."

I started to laugh. "Taj—"

"You owe me a raincheck, and I need it. We're nowhere near my parent's room. Besides, they both take Ambien. You could run a parade through their room right now, and they wouldn't wake up, Evonne."

"Okay, okay. Hand me the condom."

Taj sat up, laying the package he'd been holding in my palm. I ripped it open, tossing the wrapper behind me while he pulled off his sweatpants. Like the night before, his newly freed erection bobbed, ready for me to roll the condom on.

When it was secure, I scooted back and further up onto the bed, but when Taj followed, he laid down beside me. I moved to my knees, then straddled his body and settled on top of him, grinding on the rigid length between my thighs.

"You're the one that wants it, but I gotta ride?"

"You don't gotta."

"But you want me to."

He showed off those pearly whites, rolling his hips up. "You don't wanna ride TDub from Guys Next Door?"

I laughed at the throwback from our earlier conversation about his group nickname. "I don't know if I want to ride TDub. I wouldn't mind riding Taj Wright, though."

I bent to kiss him, catching his bottom lip between my teeth. "But you're gonna have to say the words, Nurse Dude."

"The words?"

"The *words*."

"The words that'll make you sit on my dick?" He tapped my thighs with the pads of his fingers. "Now's your chance to ride that mustang, baby. Giddy up!"

"Not exactly the passionate declaration I was going for."

"I'm playin'. Unless you're gonna do it…"

"Oh, I'm gonna do it, Nurse Dude."

———

The sun hadn't even come up when Taj tapped my thigh, nudging me awake. I was warm and comfortable, snuggled under a light blanket and crisp sheets, Taj's chest at my back, and the rest of his warmth plastered up against me, hip to toe. His arm had been slung across my waist before he gave me a few taps with the palm of his hand.

"What time is it?"

"Early. But we have to get up. Got to be somewhere."

I burrowed deeper into the cocoon of blankets, trying to savor the last bit of sleep I could get, but Taj was already moving. Cold air blew in through the space he'd left, snaking down my back. After sweaty sex and a shower, we'd been too tired to put pajamas on, so we rolled into bed naked.

"Vonne. C'mon." Taj flipped on the lamp on his side of the bed. I groaned at the intrusion of even the soft light of the low-watt bulb. "I got something to show you."

He pulled at the covers, pulling them down and exposing my nudity to the cold air of the room. He bent over me, dropping soft feather kisses down my body until I rolled onto my back, grabbed him by his cheeks, and brought his lips to mine.

"I guess you're not worried about morning trash mouth today?"

I gasped, then frowned, my brows knit together. "Oh! Oh,

no. I brushed last night—" I sat up, swinging my feet to the rug next to the bed.

"Evonne! You're..." Taj laughed, grabbing for me. He crawled across the bed, then kissed me again. "You're fine. But since you're sitting upright, get dressed. I'm taking you somewhere."

"Where are we going before sunrise?"

"It's a surprise. But I know it'll take you forever to get ready, so—"

I glared, then got up to grab my suitcase and pick out my clothes for the day. "You know what, Nurse Dude? Do not get me started on how long I waited for you yesterday."

Taj laughed, going for his suitcase as well. "Okay, you're right. I do take my time. But two divas in that bathroom is going to be interesting."

A short time later, we tiptoed out of the quiet house and got into the car. Taj backed out of the driveway and headed out of the subdivision. The first inkling of dawn was beginning to peek across the horizon.

After a few turns, we arrived at a small white building in a deserted strip mall. Then I noticed the Drunken Donuts sign out front, and everything about why we were out so early made sense.

"C'mon. We'll grab a couple of dozen."

We strolled into the small bakery where the air was warm, thick with the scent of fresh ground coffee, sugary pastries, and baking dough. The whole place smelled good enough to eat.

"Oh, good God! I don't even remember the last time I saw you, man!"

A thin man stood upfront, a hand outstretched to Taj, the grin splitting his face in half, it was so full. His blue eyes twinkled, and his face flushed pink as he rushed around the counter. His apron was stark white, as was his uniform, white polo with the Drunken Donuts logo on the left breast and knee-length cargo shorts. The two exchanged hearty hand-shakes, then back-slapping hugs and gusts of laughter.

"What the hell are you doin' back in this town?" His Alabama accent tinged every word; he sounded like the friendliest guy you'd ever meet. He planted his hands on his hips, his eyes bouncing from me to Taj and back. "*Ohhh*. I get it. Bringing a friendly *neighbor* to see the old stomping grounds, huh?"

Taj chuckled, swiping a hand across the scratchy remnants of beard that he hadn't shaved off. "Not exactly. This is Evonne." He dropped an arm across my shoulder and tucked me in close to him. "She is *actually* my neighbor, up in Potter Lake. But uh, we …uh…"

He looked at me. I looked at him. Neither of us knew what to call whatever it was we were doing. Dating, but not really? More than fuck buddies, but not much more?

"Anyway, Vonne, this is Ryan McCann. He owns the place. We went to high school together."

"Sort of," Ryan said, almost laughing.

"What does sort of mean?" I asked.

"Well, Ryan and I were at Jacksonville Cancer Center together, and we…well…"

Ryan laughed, his eyes twinkling again. "Don't try to dress it up. We had the same oncologist, and we were on the same chemo schedule, so we'd meet up. Since we were both behind in school, we went through this program run by Jacksonville Schools. It was like part home-school, part independent study. We helped each other through it. Then this guy went off to college while I became a degenerate."

"Yeah, well… you cleaned yourself up."

"Thanks to you." He tapped Taj on the arm, then turned to me. "Treatment tapped my parents out. Taj said if I could apply myself and figure out what I wanted to do, he would help me. A couple of months later, I enrolled at the community college, got my degree. My mom makes homemade donuts all the time. I thought, you know, what if we opened up a little shop together?"

He shrugged. "I floated an idea. Taj sent me a check, wouldn't take no for an answer, didn't want to be paid back. Said he wanted to see me up and running by the time he made it back to Jacksonville. And here we are," he finished, doing a full turn around the shop. It was cute and clean, white with bright pops of yellows and blues.

"And business is good."

"Oh, business is booming," he corrected, beaming. "I'm thinking about opening another location."

"If you do, consider Potter Lake, Georgia. If only to have a shop near me."

"Not even joking, that's a great thought. From what your mom says, that town is exploding. She's always in here to buy donuts to send up to you."

"Speaking of, Evonne and I finished off that last batch. I want to get a couple dozen for the house and another dozen to take home. Just give us your best mix."

"Coming right up!" Ryan ducked back behind the counter, pulled out a few white boxes, and began to fill them with a wide assortment.

Taj reached for his wallet in the back pocket of the dark blue jeans he wore. "I don't want to hear any of that *no charge* bullshit you try to pull on me. You don't make money and open franchise locations by giving the product away. We're paying for these, so ring me up."

"If you say so. But your first dozen in Potter Lake is on me."

Taj paid for the donuts and two large cups of coffee, gave Ryan another hug and handshake, and led me out of the store. We each held a bag with two dozen Drunken Donuts, which we placed on the backseat, then got into the car.

"We've got donuts. We've got coffee. Let's roll." Taj

pressed the ignition button and rolled out of the parking lot, headed to the highway. "We'll be late for our date."

"Our date?"

"Yeah." He nodded, glancing over at me between watching the road and the cars around us. "About time we had an official date, don't you think?"

After a few minutes, we passed a highway sign, and I realized we were driving east toward the coast. I smiled, bringing the cup of piping hot coffee to my lips.

"What are you smiling at, over there?" Taj asked, his head swiveling from the open road before us to me in the passenger seat.

"You need to watch the road and not me, Nurse Dude."

"You be so mean to me, Miss Girard." I realized he hadn't called me *Miss Girard* lately, and I'd missed it, a little.

"Fine. I'm smiling because it seems we are headed to the beach."

"Uh huh, we are."

"And because despite being awakened at ass-thirty o'clock in the morning—"

"Ass-thirty o'clock..."

"It was nice of you to drag me out to pick up coffee and donuts and drive me to the beach."

"My pleasure." Taj reached across the center console and grabbed my hand, threading his fingers through mine.

"And because I liked meeting your friend back there. You did a good thing for him."

Taj rolled his bottom lip between his teeth and chewed on it for a few moments. "I wanted to see him win. To get that far and fight that hard..." He was deep in thought, caught up in that time ten years in the past. "I could help him. So I did."

"He obviously appreciates it. Who knows where he'd be if you hadn't have stepped in?"

"I guess. He did the work, though. I wrote a check."

"I bet cousins you didn't know about have been crawling out of the woodwork."

"Nah, not really." He shook his head, shrugging a shoulder. "Once I dropped out of the group, most folks assumed I wouldn't be making any money. Nobody pays attention to who writes the songs. They have no idea that I get paid to write hits for a music group. And I don't tell them. The only people that need to know are my family, my friends, and the IRS."

"I hear you. Sometimes..." A derisive chuckle escaped. "Sometimes, people make you feel obligated to help. To give and to make sacrifices. Sometimes people do that on your behalf, even if you didn't ask them to do that for you. Then hold it over your head when you're not grateful for everything they did."

"Obligation is no reason to do something good. It should come from the heart."

"I mean, I agree with that. I didn't always get the choice. Sometimes it was required. Sometimes it was assumed that that was what you owed for someone else's sacrifice."

"You getting personal on me, Vonne?"

I sighed, sipping more coffee. We passed signs for Neptune Beach. The coast was coming into view, off in the distance. My heart lifted at the anticipation of watching the sun rise in the sky with the sound of ocean waves in my ears.

In the arms of someone that cared enough to bring me there.

"I was. But I'm going to let it go and enjoy myself. As you said, I should appreciate where I am right now and think about where I want to go from here. I can only go up, right?"

"Right," he answered, nodding deeply. Then repeated, "It's only... *up* from here."

twenty-two

. . .

EVONNE

"You don't know this one? How do you not know this song, Evonne?"

The strains of an upbeat song with heavy bass pounded through the surround sound in Taj's car. Four young-sounding but appealing voices sang in perfect harmony about taking rides into space, probably to meet a girl.

I shrugged. "I didn't pay any attention."

"You were too good for boy groups, huh? Probably into Aerosmith or Dave Matthews Band or something like that."

"Don't come for my black card because I didn't listen to your lil friends. I wasn't into the group. They weren't my speed. Don't take it personally."

"I'm not." He did seem offended, slightly. He pulled into a spot at the public beach off of the access walkway. "I'm surprised, is all."

The sun rose while we were in the car, drinking coffee and eating donuts. The beach was quiet, empty and serene. Taj and I sat and watched the water, the birds circling and calling each other and drank the last of our coffee in peaceful silence.

Two hurricanes a year apart had destroyed much of the pier, limiting access to the shoreline, but we made the best of it. Taj toted a box of donuts and the blanket we'd used the day before. I carried our coffee, and we set up on a small patch of grass beyond the sandy expanse that led to the surf rushing in and out.

It was *perfect*.

Except Taj seemed fitfully quiet. Deep in thought, folding and unfolding his legs, staring into the distance and chewing on his bottom lip.

"Do you want to talk about it? Or did you want to chew through your lip first?"

"Talk about what?" He asked like he hadn't been sending out *ask me what's wrong* signals for an hour.

"About whatever has you chewing your lip, for one." I considered then that maybe he didn't want to talk about it with his neighbor. I was virtually a stranger. One whose body he knew pretty well by now but still a stranger.

"If you want," I said, following up. "If not, I understand. I'll let it go. I thought you might want to—"

"Evonne." Taj tipped his head back, closed his eyes, and laughed. "You're a lot of fun."

"But?"

"But nothing." He nudged me with his elbow. "You're a lot of fun. I'm having a good time. I'm glad I invited you."

"I guess you had the choice not to. I'm glad you did, too." I leaned over and kissed him.

"Especially because that can happen now."

I laughed. "Does flirting mean you don't want to talk about it?"

He sucked in a deep breath, barreling his chest. Then exhaled slowly. "You know when people talk about worlds colliding? Past and present, work and personal?"

"I guess. Is that happening for you right now?"

"Seeing Ryan again, thinking about Ms. Doris retiring brings my past back up. I keep thinking about how much time has passed since I was fighting for my life. I'm thankful, you know? That I could fight. That my parents had insurance, even though it didn't cover everything. That I could find a way to be a part of Guys Next Door, which gave me the money to pay off those bills when they came. I got to go to school, I got a job at a brand new facility, and I'm a good... nah, I'm a *great* nurse—"

"A little mouthy, bedside manner leaves something to be desired..."

"I knew you'd have something to say about that, *Miss Girard.*"

"'Course I did, *Nurse Dude.*"

"Anyway, I'm saying I went through all of that, and it cost a lot of money. It took a lot of time and work. Blood, sweat, actual tears. It was maybe three years before I felt safe that I was cancer-free, and it wouldn't pop back. I like where I am."

His long pause was filled with the sounds of the surf and the gulls circling above. I waited. And waited.

And finally, he said, "What if there's more, though? And what if *more* doesn't have anything to do with all that work and all that money?"

"You mean... what if all that was for nothing?"

He heaved a long, loud sigh. "I have an opportunity staring me in the face. Something I didn't think would come around again. Something I could jump right into if I could work it out."

"Something work-wise?"

He paused, then nodded. "I wouldn't necessarily have to stop what I'm doing, but it would put a pause button on it for sure. But I became a nurse for a reason, and I can't abandon that. I'm not doing anything if I'm not nursing."

My heart dropped in my chest at the realization of what

he was talking about. I made an assumption, but I wanted to be sure. I *needed* to be sure because if I was right, it could mean changes for whatever it was Taj and I were doing.

"To be clear and so we're not talking in circles and metaphors, do you mean Guys Next Door?"

"I haven't made any decisions," he blurted, his words a rushing, rapid stream, as if he was trying to reassure me, or himself, of something. "There's talk. Chatter. About updating our old stuff, and they want me to work with them on it. I haven't seen the guys in over a year. We haven't sung together since I was a teenager. What if our voices don't mesh like they used to? What if…"

"Taj! Whoa. You're getting way ahead of yourself. You can only make decisions on absolutes. You don't know anything about anything yet. And what about Terrell? I thought he replaced you."

"They're kicking Terrell out to add me back in. That's what the meeting this weekend is about."

The sense of relief that rushed through me. I was almost ashamed that I wasn't going to be forced to tell him I'd slept with a member of his group.

I reached for his hand and squeezed it. "Is this something you want and you're trying to talk yourself out of? Or something you're trying to talk yourself into because the rest of them want it?"

"Good question. I don't know. That's what I've been struggling with."

Taj rolled his wrist to check at his watch and hopped up, gathering our garbage and our shoes. "Sorry to cut our date short, but we've gotta roll. I'm supposed to hit Ms. Doris' retirement party. It starts at noon."

We stomped through the seagrass and the sand back to the public beach parking lot.

Inside, I warred with myself.

I should come clean about Terrell, for the sake of honesty.

He had shared a part of himself that was not public. He had trusted me with that piece of his past.

Did I trust him with mine?

————

"Is that Lil' Taj? That can't be Lil' Taj Wright!"

"I haven't been Lil Taj in a long time, Ms. Doris."

He moved toward her, arms open and smiling wide, then folded her into a tight embrace. She patted his back and began to cry. Taj didn't release her until she settled down again and when they pulled apart, he clutched her gnarled hands and stepped back.

Ms. Doris, who Taj said had always been tall and thin, was a withered shell of a woman in a knee-length white dress. She stood next to a round table decorated with a spray of brightly colored flowers and white tablecloths. The room was teeming with people, some young, some older, some in scrubs, some in spring dresses. Jazz music overhead hummed over the din of conversation.

"You're not looking too bad, young lady. On your feet and moving around. I know you haven't let a few years slow you down any. Still giving people a hard time, you ole battle-ax."

"You know it's my way, Taj. I just moved into this place." She waved a hand into the air, indicating the ballroom of the Assisted Living facility. "And immediately had to take over the Activities Coordinator work. They were doing a poor job of getting the residents up and moving. It's important to keep active."

She shook her silver head with her eyes closed. Then she opened them and gave him the biggest, brightest smile, all of her teeth on display. "It's so lovely to see you! I sent a note to your mom, but I didn't think you'd come down here for this. She told me you got a *good* job, and you bought a house and everything. You must be so busy with your nursing and home projects."

"You know I wouldn't miss this celebration for the world."

"Well, you sit right here at my table...*ohhh.*" She then stepped clean around him, planting a fist in her slight hip. "You cheatin' on me, ain't you? With this young, pretty gal here, I suppose."

Taj laughed, tightening his grasp on my hand in his. I was so relieved that I'd thrown in a tea-length, off the shoulder dress into my suitcase at the last minute. I didn't know why, but I needed to make a good impression on this woman.

"I'm sorry, Ms. Doris. Yes, I am. This is Evonne Girard, my date."

"Well, I guess it's all right, so long as she's a nice gal. Is you? A nice gal?"

The flash of panic on Taj's face was amusing, but I was a natural at talking to people. My clientele at the Curl & Dye was mostly over sixty. The older patrons I served had the best stories and loved to gossip.

"You know Taj wouldn't choose a woman who didn't treat him like you would," I said, talking over whatever Taj was about to say in my defense. "I've got this on lock, Ms. Doris."

I held out my fist, which Ms. Doris promptly bumped. The smile on her lips was a small, proud one. She reminded me a little of Grandma Bobbie, which made me miss her.

"Now tell me, Ms. Doris, about how many years did you work as a nurse?"

"'Bout forty-five years, give or take, here and there. Some emergency, some floor nursing, but I spent most of my career in oncology. Cancer ward, you know. Mmmhmm..." She paused for a breath, then went on. "Did some Palliative and Hospice Care for a little bit in there..."

"Oh, Ms. Doris. But you didn't stay in that field?"

"Nope," she answered quickly and fiercely. "It weren't for

me. I need to guide that daily journey. The fight, not the ride home to glory. Respect it. Couldn't do it."

"I'm sure it's a blessing to know where you belong and what you're supposed to be doing." I slid a glance over at Taj, who gave me the slightest of nods. He heard me. And he got it, I hoped.

"Truth be told, I sure feel like I could work more, but this arthritis got me all bound up." She grimaced, opening and closing her hands, knobby with swollen joints. "They say I got to sit down, let the young ones earn their due."

"That gives you plenty of time to train Nurse Wright, then. I met Taj when I visited his clinic, and I feel like he could use a good talking-to from a professional."

"Don't let that beautiful face fool you. She was impossible."

"Sounds a lot like yourself," Ms. Doris shot back, her red lips pursed. She hooked her arm into mine and guided us to the seats next to her at the table. "She can sit next to me. We can gossip about how you liked to mess with your monitors and would refuse to eat unless I was on shift, to get on my nerves."

"That does sound like something Taj would do," I said, settling into the seat next to her.

"Why we gotta bring up old stuff, though, Ms. Doris?" Taj dropped into a seat. He reached for a glass of iced tea and a few packets of sugar, ripped them open and dumped them into the glass, then stirred with a spoon. He sipped his tea and listened to me charm Ms. Doris, regaling her with the story of how Taj and I had met.

After she got up to greet more guests to her party, Taj slid an arm across the back of my chair, leaned in, and kissed my bare shoulder. "You are a goddamn delight. I'm so glad you're here," he said. Then he went back to drinking iced tea and scrolling his phone.

The party was as lovely as I imagined it would be and

then some, a fitting send-off to a career nurse who had treated hundreds of patients and trained so many nurses. I met more than a few former patients who had come to honor Ms. Doris and a few former staff members that had worked with her.

And Taj had already been roped into a commitment to visit her and make sure she was well.

"Then I can check on your technique and bedside manner myself. And bring her with you," she demanded, angling a thumb in my direction.

"I will," he promised, which was a surprise to me. I knew full well that I probably wouldn't be accompanying him on his next visit to Jacksonville.

When the party started to break up because Ms. Doris needed a nap, Taj and I left. After he tucked me into the car, he walked around and dipped into the driver's seat, then pressed the ignition button. I leaned over the center console and brushed my lips across his cheek.

"What was that?"

I shrugged, settling back into the molded leather seat. "I had a good time. And you're adorable."

He reached for the gear shift, then paused, pulling back. "Really? You liked that old lady gang going on in there?"

"What? She was hilarious! Especially all of her Lil Taj stories. She makes *me* want to be a nurse."

He groaned, this time putting the car in gear and pulling out of the spot. "Yeah, I noticed you two bonding over your mutual love of picking on me."

"Aw, she does love you."

"Unh huh. That's a sign of love, is it?"

He wanted me to joke around about how picking on him was a sign of love and somehow correlate it to how much we playfully bickered. But there was no telling how that would end up.

Either I would let myself admit that I did actually care about Taj, and I wouldn't mind something real with him.

Or he would use the opportunity to remind me that what we had was some fun, something to do, not to get attached, otherwise, like he'd tossed Jaslene to the side for me, he could toss me aside for someone else.

You can lose them like you got them. I wasn't about to go out like that.

I didn't answer. And Taj didn't prod. Instead, he turned up the music and bopped his head to the bass thumping through the sound system.

twenty-three

· · ·

EVONNE

I laid back on the bed, actively ignoring the pile of clothing I'd peeled off of my body.

Taj and I had had a full day, from sunrise at the beach to an afternoon with geriatric nurses. I was supposed to be getting dressed for dinner, but while Taj was filling his parents in on Ms. Doris' retirement party, I stole away for a few minutes to myself.

To think. To try and regain a tenuous grasp on what this weekend was supposed to be about—escaping Potter Lake, getting to know Taj, having a good time.

Don't turn it into more, I lectured. If Taj goes back to Guys Next Door...

My phone pulsed from somewhere underneath me. I dragged my bag out and rifled through it, trying to catch the call before it rolled to voicemail.

"Hello."

"Girl, where are you?"

I sat up, almost jumping out of my skin. I hadn't even

checked the screen; I'd assumed it was someone I wanted to talk to. My mother never called me. *Ever*.

"Mama! What do you mean, where am I?"

"All of the news reports are saying Potter Lake was destroyed in the storm. Ebony said you told her you were fine, but you didn't see fit to call your parents, so we drove on out here."

My eyes bugged out. Instead of calling me? They hopped in the car and drove twenty miles west?

"Well, the salon is a mess. Don't seem like you'll be working there for a while, so how you're going to pay rent, I don't know. The one girl that was there said you'd probably be at home, so we drove over here. Your car is here, but you are not. I don't understand what's going on, Evonne."

My eyes slid closed, and I shook my head slowly. This wasn't about my safety. She was trying to catch me doing something she didn't want me doing.

"I'm in Jacksonville with—"

The door flew open, and Taj rushed in. "Hey, sorry. Our reservation is for 7 o'clock. Let's hop in the shower together, save some ti—oh." He flinched as he realized I was on the phone, then mouthed, "Sorry," and bent to unzip his suitcase.

"— a friend of mine..." I finished. His head popped up, and he winked.

"Friend?" My mother screeched so loud I had to pull the phone away from my ear. "What kind of *friend* wants you to get in the shower with him?"

"Mama, what do you need?"

"I *need* to know why my daughter is in Jacksonville with some man we don't know."

I almost laughed, but she would explode. "There are men in my life that you don't know."

Terrell. Jerome. Taj. All the men at the barbershop, for starters.

"Do not get smart with me, Evonne. You know your mouth doesn't amuse me."

"I'm not trying to get smart. I'm fine; I'm safe, I'm alive. My landlord was headed out of town for the weekend, and I caught a ride. That's all—"

"You must think I'm stupid. That man asked you to get in the shower. And he's your landlord, you said? So that's how you're paying rent while you're not working?"

For a full three or four seconds, I wasn't sure I'd heard what I heard.

And then I knew that I had heard what I'd heard.

And I snapped.

"You know what, Mama? If you want to believe that my landlord asks me to sleep with him in exchange for a place to live, then yes, this is how I pay my rent. Not with the money I earned at my two jobs because I'm good at what I do."

"Who do you think you're talking to? These choices are why it was not a good idea for you to move out. You'd best find a greyhound or an airline and bring your fast tail back—"

Derisively, loudly, disrespectfully, I laughed.

"No, Mama. I'm not running home because you said so. I'm a fully grown, responsible adult. I'm on my own; I pay my rent with the money that I *earn*. I'm hanging up now because I have to get in the shower with a handsome, sexy, delicious spectacle of a man that you don't know so that we can make our dinner reservation."

I ended the call and threw the phone across the room, flinging myself back onto the bed. It bounced off of the edge of Taj's suitcase, where he kneeled over it, staring hard.

"Was that your mother?"

"Don't patronize me. You heard my side of that conversation. You know it was her."

"Well… maybe she…"

I shot back up with my mouth set to flame him. "Do not

take up for her! She fully meant to insinuate that I'm fucking you to pay the rent."

"I'm not going to talk shit about your mom, Evonne. I just…" He shrugged and seemed not to know what to say.

I didn't know what I wanted him to say. I didn't know if I wanted him to say anything.

He came to the bed, then flopped down beside me. I didn't say a word, while the tears slid down my cheeks.

"Are you okay?"

I sniffled. "No."

My phone rang again. It was either my mother or my sister, and I wasn't in the mood for any Girard's.

"I'll cancel our reservation. Lasagna is better the second night, anyway. We'll watch a movie. I'll let you beat my ass at some game you don't even know how to play."

I let out a whimper and tucked my head into the space between his head and shoulder. "I didn't want to ruin your plans for tonight."

He kissed my forehead, then dipped to take a light but long detour to my lips. "You're here. With me. That's all I care about."

He pulled his phone from his pocket. I watched while he logged into a reservations app, clicked on the 7 PM slot, and pressed cancel. Once it was confirmed, the phone buzzed. He slid the phone back into his pocket, then wrapped both arms around me.

"Why would she say that, Taj? Just… what the fuck? Who says that?"

"I don't know, babe. But don't drive yourself crazy trying to figure it out. You are hundreds of miles away from all of that, remember? Leave it there."

Taj's hands were heavy, which made his long passes down my arm, up and down my back with the occasional pat more comforting than I was prepared for it to be. Anymore cuddling with my landlord and I would mess around and *like him*.

I got up from the bed and went into the bathroom to start the shower. My hands still shook so furiously that I could barely turn the knobs. When hot water sprayed a steady stream from the shower head, I slammed the door shut, hooked my thumbs into the band of my panties, and shimmied them down my hips.

"Hey," I called to Taj, whose long form still laid on the bed, shoes and all. Taj lowered the phone. His eyebrows rose at the sight of my exposed curves, full breasts, taut nipples.

"Come in here with me."

He rolled off the bed, already kicking off his shoes and unbuttoning the crisp white shirt he'd worn to the party. He unzipped his slacks and yanked them down, kicking them toward his suitcase.

I disappeared around the corner and into the shower. Moments later, he joined me, pulling me up against him. I wrapped my arms around his body and let the tears come, hard and fast.

He let me cry until I was done. Then he kissed the last of the tears away.

After a delicious dinner of leftover lasagna, a spirited discussion of all the ways that Love & Basketball was a terrible movie with Theresa and Randall, and some time answering website email, I closed the lid of my laptop.

Then picked up the phone, mindlessly scrolling messages and Instagram. My mother hadn't emailed or texted or called to say she was sorry. I didn't expect her to; Rhonda Girard was never sorry.

Taj took the laptop and snatched the phone from my fingers, setting them on the nightstand, then crawled into bed next to me. Without thinking, I snuggled up against him. His arms came to rest around me.

"This feels good," he said. "This right here. With you."

I looked at up him. He looked down at me.

"We are about to be in trouble, aren't we, Miss Girard?"

"As fuck, Nurse Dude."

———

She didn't mean it, Vonne. She was trying to find a weakness in your armor, so you're back under her control.

I awoke to a text from my sister that I tried to ignore. I grabbed the phone and rolled toward Taj, who slept on his side facing me. He didn't snore, but he did breathe hard and heavy. I knew by the steadiness of his breath that he was still asleep, but the vibration of the phone against wood awakened me from the lightest of snoozes.

I swiped the message open and moved my thumbs across the screen. *What did you hear, and from who?*

Three bubbles appeared. I waited for Ebony to answer back. *Grandma Bobbie was in the car. You know she tells everything.*

I giggled, trying to stay quiet. *That big mouth ole lady.*

Ebony wrote back: *Said she laid into Mama like you don't know what. Told her she was evil and needed to go pray! Daddy was like, Mama settle down back there but she kept talking all the way back to Healy cause they couldn't make her shut up.*

I laughed harder, shaking the bed with the effort to not make a sound. Taj stirred but didn't wake up.

Daddy sad something too, about how she needs to let up on you. That she's the reason you moved out. Mama ain't said a word since they got home.

She's slamming stuff around though so I'm hiding in the basement. About to go into work for some extra hours to get out of here.

The thought that Fearless Ebony was hiding to not be around her made my heart sink. Maybe my mother was an angry person with high expectations that were never met, that lashed out to stay in control, but I was more than sure she'd never want her children to avoid her very presence. Or, at least, she shouldn't want that.

Well, get up and get to work. You have a savings account to pad. :) When the power is back on in Potter Lake, you can come stay with me when you need a break.

K, I'm getting up. And count on a house guest when you're back in town. Tell Nurse Dude I said heyyy.

I pressed the button to lock the phone and lobbed it to the end of the bed since I didn't want to roll over again, then settled back into the warm, comfortable spot I'd been in earlier.

Taj's eyes were open. I hadn't noticed that his breathing had become lighter. He gave me a sleepy half-smile. "Sorry to disturb your text conversation with my REM sleep cycle."

"I'm sorry," I whispered, snuggling up against his warm body, wrapping my arms around his torso. "Didn't mean to wake you up. Go back to sleep."

"Uhm…." He pulled me closer, then hooked a hand in the bend of my leg and pulled until it was slung across his body, and I was right up against him. Taj slept in the nude, so there was no missing his arousal between us. "How am I supposed to go back to sleep with you here?"

He teased me, rubbing the head of his dick against my clit, then dipped to my slit to soak the tip with my moisture, then back up. I cupped his face and brought his mouth to mine. He hummed a pleasured moan, dipping to brush his lips across my cheek, my ears, my shoulders.

"I like how fast we moved past you not kissing me in the morning."

"I kiss you in the morning!"

"Not before having a fit about your breath, you don't."

I smirked, then looped my arms around his neck. "If you can't take me at my morning mouth, you don't deserve me at my morning sex."

"Is that what's about to happen?"

"How many condoms did you bring?"

"Enough," he growled, then snapped his teeth at my bottom lip. "How are you?"

I didn't want to answer. Not because I didn't want to talk about it, but because I didn't know how I was. Instead, I gyrated my pelvis and ground against him.

"Do you really want to talk right now?"

"Nope."

He sat up a little, giving us some room to pull at the nightshirt bunched up around my thighs. I helped, raising my body enough to pull the cotton fabric up and over my head. He threw it over the side of the bed, reached to the end table for the pile of condoms he had tossed there, and lowered his body to mine again.

Taj wasn't slight, but he wasn't a big man, either. I craved the sheer weight of him, though, pressing me into the mattress. The way his warmth pushed into me, sweat dripping and mingling with mine, the way the muscles in his legs, his arms, his back tensed and relaxed as he moved. He pulsed with energy. I got off on his raw sexual need and that he sought me to satisfy him.

Whoever said sex didn't fix things never had sex with Taj Wright. Those moments when we were joined was everything I needed, precisely when I needed it.

Taj exhaled, kissed my forehead, and rolled away, muttering something about dealing with the condom. I snatched up the scarf that had come off of my hair and dropped it onto the side table, then pushed myself to a sitting position and raked my fingers through my hair.

"What's that face for?" Taj asked, sauntering out of the bathroom. "Do we need another go around? We have plenty of condoms." He slid back into the bed and pulled the sheets up around his chest.

"You planned to get really lucky, huh? How many *did* you bring?"

"Enough," he growled again, hooking my elbow and pulling me toward him. I sidled up against him and laid my head on his chest. He wrapped both arms around me. "Feel like answering that question now?"

"What question?"

"How are you? Yesterday was rough on you. This is Nurse Taj, randomly checking you for a fever."

I flipped over so I could see him. "Right now? At this precise moment?" I grinned, then poked the tip of my finger into the dimple on his chin. "I'm pretty fucking good. Emphasis on the *fucking*."

"Seriously, Evonne."

"What, Taj? What do you want me to say? You fucked all the anger out? You made me come twice, so I'm not thinking about how my mother ruined my day?"

I pulled the covers back in an attempt to sit up, but he tightened his grip on me, intertwining his arms with mine.

"I'll tell you what I don't want you to say. I don't want you to try to be funny. I don't want you to ramble about nothing, and I don't want you to tell me about any podcasts. I want you to be real with me."

I huffed, then laid back. "I'm fine. Seriously, I'm fine. She's always been like that. It hurts for a little while, then she'll make nice, and everything will be fine. And then something will make her mad..."

"Always? Your whole life?"

"Always. It's cyclic." I nodded, raising my eyes to his. "I have spent so many years trying to make her happy. Getting the grades, doing extra work, jumping when she says to jump. Spelman was about making her happy. If I would have kept my eyes on the prize, not tried to act grown, not been distracted by—"

"Well, you know what we say about the past—"

"But I need to tell you something about Spelman, about that guy that I dated. He's—"

"You don't need to go through any of that again. It's in the past; it's *ten years* in the past. You can't rehash this over and over again. It'll drive you crazy."

"I'm not rehashing. Seriously, there's something I never told you—"

"There's nothing I need to know about a man that sucked up all your innocence, dumped you, and let you twist in the wind when you got into trouble. Nothing."

He kissed me, then gave me a brief nod, like that was the end of it. But it couldn't be the end of it.

He sat up, bringing me with him. "Let's get some coffee. I think my mom is up. She likes to make a big breakfast because she thinks I don't eat enough."

"Taj…"

"Evonne, let it go." Taj stepped into a pair of soft cotton lounge pants and tied the strings at the waistband. "Just for the weekend. Let it all go."

I huffed and rolled out of bed. "Fine. I didn't want to talk about his ass anyway."

twenty-four

. . .

TAJ

"Yo, I think I could have been a rapper. I can spit rhymes. On this next album y'all should let me—"

"Nah, Yung Dav. Lil Davon. You can't rap on our next album. We're tryna keep our fans."

"Shut up, Quise. I got bars."

"You got bars like a white dude."

"So? Logic is a white dude. Eminem is a white dude."

"You got bars like a *not cool* white dude. You don't even have Beastie Boys bars."

I burst into the cozy den at Cash's parent's place, surprising the group of men in sweats and t-shirts seated around the sparsely furnished room. Most of the house had already been packed up, with the den being the last room in the house with furniture in it. Fitting, since that was where we'd always hang out, back in the day.

"I know this Post Malone, Macklemore, 3rd Bass sounding muhfuckah is not talking about rapping on a Guys Next Door track. Not on my watch!"

They exploded in gut-level shouts and hopped up from the couches, crowding me in the most joyous, if not an ear-splitting cacophony of noise.

"Bro-ceephus!" Yelled Cash, his face split with his wide smile. He lifted a hand to me; I clasped it and pulled him into a hug. I hadn't seen him in nearly a year. It was long past time for handshakes.

"Bro-diciousness! Sup, Cash. What are y'all doing?"

"We're chillin'. Definitely wasn't sure we'd see you. How'd you get in here?"

"You left the door unlocked. And just in time; I heard Dav talking about rapping." I turned to him, my arms open to hug him even as I was admonishing him. "Sorry, LL Cool Dav, You don't have bars. Trust."

"I want to spread my wings, but y'all some haters." He clapped my back to end our hug and pulled back to get a good look. "Looking fresh, looking real good. Glad you could make the meeting. But uh…"

He stroked a weak, barely-there goatee. "Who… is *that*?" He strolled at what he probably thought was a seductive speed across the room, toward Evonne.

I hadn't told her where we were going, just that we were taking a walk. She was likely still in shock at being in the same room with some music industry heavy hitters. The net worth of the room climbed into the hundreds of millions, but you'd never know it from the unshaven faces and casual attire.

Still, egos didn't take a day off, and I didn't want Davon to do any damage.

"Aht!" I held out my palm, pressing against his chest. "She's with me. Down boy."

"You're blockin' a brother hard, Taj."

"Because you need to go on and back up, Dav."

"She's with you? You sure?"

"Positive. Don't you have a girl?"

Dav sucked his teeth and wandered back to his seat. "I'm dating, not dead."

"Evonne, these are my friends. Corey, who we call Cash cause he's good with numbers and his dad is an accountant; Marquise, who we call Quise cause his name has too many letters in it, and you met our Mack Daddy Davon. We call him Dav because he was jealous that he didn't have a nickname. Y'all, this is Evonne."

She smiled, shaking hands all around.

"She's from Potter Lake. That storm we had knocked out power for most of the town. I didn't want to leave her to sit in the dark, so I bought her home."

"You brought her to Jacksonville," said Cash, "to hang out with old people and meet some big heads you used to know? You've lost your edge, TDub."

"Taj has been a perfect host," said Evonne. "I'm loving Jacksonville, and I got to see the ocean for the first time."

"Evonne isn't impressed by Guys Next Door. I showed her my trophy room, and she yawned…"

"Stop it, Taj. I did not yawn!"

"She also had never heard Space Cowboy before I played it for her yesterday."

"Sounds like you got a real one to me," said Cash.

"Yeah, she's a real one. I was going to set her up somewhere while we meet, okay?"

"I don't need an escort. I'll find a spot far, far away." She pulled her bag open and brought out her phone, a set of Bluetooth earbuds, and a paperback book. "Don't mind me. I'll just catch up on my favorite podcast."

"Don't scare the shit out of yourself. You know how you get after you listen to that murder podcast."

"Shut up, Nurse Dude."

She smirked, then went back the way we'd come. I watched her walk into the empty living room and sit on the brick hearth in front of the fireplace, earbuds already inserted, her fingers gliding across the screen.

"She might need some company." Dav started to get up, but I flipped him my middle finger and took the seat next to him.

"She's fine. Probably texting her sister to tell her I'm not a serial killer. That's high praise from the two of them. So…" I clapped my hands together. "Y'all been talking?"

"Yeah, man. We've been talking." Cash sat forward, his hands clasped. His skin was a lighter tone, his hair a copper hue. However light—or redbone, as media often referred to him, his bass voice had no floor. Cash could go as deep as we needed him to go. He held up the foundation of our sound.

"Anybody hear from Terrell?" Marquise asked, sipping on a venti cup of coffee. He was thinner than the last time I'd seen him, which was a good thing. Opiates upset his stomach, which drove him to eat to ease the symptoms. More use meant serious weight gain. He blew up like the Marshmallow Man. In the months since his release from rehab, he'd slimmed down a lot. He was grateful to be working and taking things a day at a time.

Davon groaned, stroking his goatee and kicking his leg out to prop it on the coffee table in front of him. "I've called, left messages, sent texts. He never replies. I say we take that as a sign that he wants no parts in this next album. If TDub is comin' back, we don't have a spot for him. I'm not splitting payday five ways."

"I… I haven't decided if I—"

"Of course TDub is coming back," said Quise, who stared at me. "That's why you're here. Right, T?" His eyes begged me to confirm his assumption.

I shook my head, splaying my hands palms up. "Guys, I… of course, I want to come back. Of course, I want to work with my friends, my brothers. Of course, I want the chance to live out that dream I used to have, to see our name in lights, up on the marquee. It's just... I have a job, a good job that I need to fall back on because I can't be grinding on the stage when I'm in my 60s. Maybe Dav can but..."

The room filled with laughter, breaking some of the tension that had built.

"I need to know what coming back means. Is it full time? Is it one album? Is it an album and a tour? That means travel and extended time off. I have a life, I have a house, I have..."

I glanced up, seeking out Evonne's form, rooms away. We'd been keeping things light since everything with her was brand new, but I already didn't want to leave her behind to travel to ten, twenty, fifty cities. To sing the same songs and dance the same moves, then escape to a hotel room at night to hold no one and be with no one, to hope I could catch her on FaceTime and capture what intimate moments we could. I didn't want a "fly her out" kind of situation.

"You act like we don't have lives, too," said Cash. "I've got kids; my parents are here. Quise has his brothers. Dav has a solo career, a girl he's getting serious about. We all have something we're risking."

"I hear you. I do." I stood, shoving my hands into my pockets. I had to move; the pressure on my chest, on my shoulders, was the heaviest I'd ever felt. "But your lives, your families are here in Jax. The studios are here; the rehearsal halls are here—"

"Whose idea was it to move four hours away, bruh?"

"I was moving on with my life, Quise. Why stick around here? Y'all replaced me—"

"Terrell was always temporary," argued Quise as he pushed up from the couch. "You knew that from jump. We stood around that hospital bed and told you that shit, so don't play this innocent, *y'all didn't have a place for me* bullshit. You always had a spot."

"When you called us that day," said Dav, "Remember we were in Memphis. You said you had that last scan, and you were good. We asked you if you wanted to come back—"

"I said no because Terrell had a contract."

"So the fuck what?" Quise shouted. "We would have broken that contract, paid him out, and said *fuck you* to that asshole. We've had to suffer all this time with this nigga that can't hit the notes right, can't make it sound right. He might linger in the right register, but the songs were arranged with TDub in mind. The voice isn't right."

"Guys... guys." Cash stood then, and because Cash was up, Dav got up, too. "Taj isn't the enemy. The goal is to see what we can do to bring him back. Terrell's contract is up, and we agree that we don't plan on signing another one with him, so the point is moot. All right?"

Cash held up his hands, palms out amidst the low rumble of male voices in the room. "Let's chill out. Everybody have a seat. Who wants a beer—"

A commotion that sounded like arguing ceased all conversation. "What is that— is that Evonne?" Cash glanced at me. "Is she on the phone?"

I shook my head. "That sounds like a guy's voice. Outside."

The four of us rushed up the short flight of stairs to the main landing, past the living room where Evonne had been sitting. Her bag was there, as was her phone and her earbuds but she was not. We followed the sound of a loud argument outside the front door.

"— fuck are you doing here, Terrell?"

A tall, hulking, ebony man stood in front of Evonne, hands in the pockets of his shorts, his black t-shirt clinging to every muscle in his torso. He moved to step closer to her.

She took a step back.

"Me? Fuck *you* doing here, Evonne? I ain't seen you in

what, ten years? Still look good, though." He gave her the once-over and nodded his head. "Fuckable."

"Ten years. Right about when you dumped me in the middle of a party you brought me to."

A deep chuckle rolled from his throat. "It's not like you were the only girl I was fucking. You were boring, so—"

Quise exploded from inside the house, sending the screen door flying against the brick exterior. "Yo, Terrell! What the fuck are you doing here?"

Terrell slowly turned, pulling his hands from his pockets. He held a jumble of keys in one hand. The other was empty. "Why do y'all keep asking me that? I have piles of texts and emails about a meeting today, bugging me to show up. I drove down from Atlanta since the three of you are so goddamn clingy. Can't do shit on your own."

He tipped his head in Evonne's direction. "Like she used to be. And probably still is. Chickenheads don't change. Which one of you is doing her? I might want one last turn at it."

"Evonne...."

I stepped in front of Marquise, whose jaw was clenched and hands were balled into fists so tightly that his knuckles were losing color. Then moved past Terrell and stood in front of Evonne. Her eyes popped from him to me.

"You *know* Terrell?"

"That's what I was trying to tell you this morning," she said. Her tone was low, near a whisper. Understandably the whole group didn't need to know she'd had a fling with their second tenor. "He was the guy from Spelman."

"That's right," he crowed proudly. "Should have known she would hook up with the sickly one. You made it through that cancer bullshit, though. Congrats, real talk. Still alive to be the corniest nigga I know."

He nodded toward Evonne. "She's good, as groupies go. She liked my money and what I could offer her. Country girls are easy like that. And she's a whore so she'll do anything you want her to—"

One moment I was standing on the porch, comforting a shaking Evonne.

The next, I cocked my fist back, whirled around, and heard the crack of bone when I popped Terrell in the jaw.

twenty-five

. . .

EVONNE

I screamed.

I didn't mean to; it tore from my throat as I watched Taj deliver a punch so hard, we all heard that sickening crunch of bone.

In the melee that followed, I was knocked out of the way, and the two ended up on the lawn, a ball of legs and arms and grunts and curses, punches and slaps, and yelps of pain. Quise, Cash, and Dav tried to jump in to stop the fight. Each of them got popped in the face for their trouble.

All down the street, front doors swung open, and neighbors stepped out onto their porches to see what the commotion was about. I saw more than one person on their phone.

Fuck. These good folks were about to call the police on the *black guys having a fistfight on the lawn*. Potter Lake and Healy were small enough to be shielded from some of the police brutality but not from the nationwide reporting of it. This was a large metropolitan city. I already knew that if the police showed up, somebody was going to jail.

Or worse.

I grabbed Taj's arm and held on for dear life, trying to pull him away from Terrell. I held him by the face to capture his attention. His eyes were practically glowing with anger.

"Stop it!" I screamed. "The police are on the way, and I swear to God if you get arrested or you die fighting this man over me…" I shook my head, letting my eyes fill with tears.

"Listen to your girl, man. For once, she's smart."

Terrell sat mere paces away, leaning back on his palms, his legs splayed out in front of him. He was filthy from the loose grass and dirt on the lawn. He had it in his hair, on his face and his jaw was already swelling from the first punch. He also had the start of a nose bleed.

Taj didn't look much better. He'd got a fist in the eye and a cut on his brow. Both were bleeding. The knuckles on one had were bloody and swollen. He panted heavily, like he'd run a mile uphill.

He glanced away, spit a glob of bloody mucus in the grass, then grumbled at me. "Help me up."

I let him lean against me so he could pull himself to his feet. He slung an arm over my shoulder and limp-walked back into the house.

Behind us, I heard Cash tell Terrell to leave and not come back.

"Oh, no doubt," Terrell said. "I only showed up to tell y'all I'm my way to Miami to record another solo album. I sell more on my own—"

"So we're on the same page," spit Marquise. "Because we don't want you back."

I heard the front door slam shut. I had walked Taj back to the den and sat him down on the couch, then went to the kitchen to see if I could find some ice.

"Cash?"

His head spun toward me like he had forgotten that I was there. His hard glare softened. I was digging ice cubes out of the bin from the automatic ice maker. "Do you have a towel or something? For Taj."

"Yeah, yeah. Lemme grab that." He disappeared up the stairs, then came back with a few towels.

I wet two, dumped a handful of ice in one, and carried both back to the den. "Here," I whispered, dotting his skin to wipe away the blood. "Do you think you need to go to the—"

Taj snatched the towel from me and took the handmade ice pack. "You can go back to where you were sitting so we can finish this meeting. Thanks."

That was a shock. I had tried that morning to tell him about Terrell, and now he was mad that he'd found out about Terrell? "Okay," I said, faux light tone to my voice. "We'll talk later."

"Actually, why don't you head back to the house? I'll be back later on." He leaned over so he could dig into his pocket and handed me the key fob to his car. "In case you need it."

Speechless, I took the key and stared at him, seeking anything in his eyes that would tell me that we were not in danger of not being 'we.' His eyes were hard and cold, though. He shut them, I guess, when he got tired of me staring at him.

I whispered goodbyes and apologies to the others, grabbed my things, and walked out of the house. The driveway was empty; Terrell had hopped into a souped-up yellow Range Rover and sped away.

I was halfway down the street when a patrol car rode past me, nice and slow. No lights, no sirens. I stood on the sidewalk and watched the car stop in front of Cash's house.

I argued with myself. I should go back. What if…

A few minutes later, the same officers walked out of the front door and got back into the cruiser.

———

"Okay, never have I ever…"

I surveyed the table of people I had collected over the hour and a half I'd been sitting at the bar. I never made it into the house; I knew Randall and Theresa would have questions, and I didn't want to explain to them why I was alone. Why Taj had gotten into a fight. Not without Taj, anyway.

I got into his car and searched the built-in GPS for any place in the vicinity where I could have a drink. I ended up at *Players*, a sports bar. After a few drinks alone, I'd been roped into a conversation with a few gentlemen sharing a booth, then invited to sit with them.

"…been to a topless beach!"

Groans sounded around the table as a few in the group slammed back shots or took drinks from ice-cold bottles.

"That was an easy one, Evonne," slurred the guy sitting next to me.

"Oh, it was, was it? Okay, Cutie, how about this one?" He'd told me his name, but I'd forgotten it and had resorted to calling him Cutie. "Never have I ever… said I loved someone to get laid."

"I've done that."

"Bottoms up!"

I giggled but didn't drink. "Who has a good one?"

"How about this one?" Offered a familiar voice from beyond the group. "Never have I ever let someone take a beating over me. Never have I ever lied to save face. Never have I ever—"

"Taj!" I bumped Cutie, prompting him to move so I could scoot out of the booth. "Sorry, guys, my… landlord is here. Continue without me!"

Moans of disappointment were drowned out by someone else taking the reins.

Taj nodded his head toward the bar, and we slipped into empty seats. He ordered two Cokes and two glasses of water and slid a twenty dollar bill across the counter, telling the bartender to keep the change. I accepted the tall glass of cola, unwrapped a straw, and sucked down a long, fizzy sip.

"Drink up. I'm not taking you home to my parents when you look and sound drunk."

"Because you look so much better?" I eyed the swelling in his face and the mangled knuckles.

"That's what I mean. They have enough to deal with."

"How did you find me?" I asked, after a few tense, thick minutes.

"I have OnStar."

Taj sucked down half of his drink, then set it down on a thin cardboard coaster bearing the bar's logo and pushed it away. His eyes drifted up toward the giant flat screens broadcasting several sporting events.

"How did you end up here, Evonne? I sent you back to the house."

"You gave me the key to the car. I wasn't supposed to use it?"

He planted an elbow on the wooden bar and went to rub his eye, then hissed from the pain. He'd forgotten about his injuries. "I expected you to be at the house, so I got there, and you weren't there, and I was worried. I called you a hundred times."

I dug my phone from my bag and gulped. The sound had been turned down so that it didn't disturb their meeting. I hadn't turned it back up, so I didn't hear any of the half dozen calls he'd made. He left a voicemail and also sent texts. The last one read:

Tracked the car. Don't go anywhere. I'm coming there.

"Well, you found me." I dropped the phone back into my bag. "You're still pissed off, though. You could have stayed at the house."

"Not when you have my car, and you've been sucking down drinks for two hours."

"I haven't... I've had *one* drink, Taj. Whiskey, if you care. If I turn into a lush, it'll be your fault."

"Why didn't I know about Terrell, Evonne?"

"I tried to tell you about his ass this morning, but you were on the *Don't Think About The Past, Leave That Shit Back There* tour."

His top lip curled. He was nearly shaking with the effort to keep his voice low. "I showed you the picture of us, and you recognized him right off. You should have told me right then."

"Maybe I needed to trust you first," I spat back.

"You told me everything about Spelman except who you were messing with. I thought we were talking about some random nigga from Atlanta. You purposely left Terrell's name out."

"As far as I'm concerned, we *were* talking about some random nigga from Atlanta. I don't give a shit about Terrell, or what group he was in. And if you would have told me about Guys Next Door before two days ago, I would have told you about Terrell."

I sucked down more cola. Watched a few minutes of TV. Watched Taj fume out of the corner of my eye.

"I thought I had more time. It's not like I wanted to admit I got suckered by a celebrity, and then knowing he's the guy that took your spot?" I exhaled, shaking my head. "I'm never interested in talking about Terrell Hawkins. What does it even matter, though? We aren't dating. We're just friends, remember?"

His head dropped until his jaw practically rested on his chest. "You and I both know we are past that point, Evonne. At least I am." He clicked his tongue and drank more from his straw. "He could have hurt you. How did you end up outside with him?"

"He pulled up, loud and obnoxious, music blasting. I could hear it over my podcast, feel the bass through the floor.

I got up to see who was being an asshole, and he hopped out. I thought I could talk him out of coming in if he saw me standing there. I told you, I wanted to punch him in the fucking forehead."

"Same," he seethed.

"He went in as soon as he saw me. Of course, I was a Neighbor. Of course, I was trying to hook up with other members of his group to get closer to him. Nobody wants his ugly ass."

"Actually," Taj interrupted, laughing a little. "He's got three babies out there by various women. Lucky you weren't one of them."

"Those women have terrible taste. I prefer my pop stars a little more humble. Along the 'TDub from Guys Next Door' variety."

I thought he would laugh, but he shook his head. "Don't," he mumbled quietly. "You weren't impressed with TDub before. Don't pretend you're impressed by him now."

"What does that mean? Now you don't want me because I fucked another member of your lil group? Don't want to come in behind Terrell again? First, he took your spot, then he took your pussy?"

Taj flinched. Then his eyes slammed shut. Even *I* knew I'd gone too far.

"That… that wasn't fair, Taj. I'm sorr—"

"We're leaving," he growled. "I was looking for you because I got a text from Potter Lake City Hall. The transformer is up. I want to check out the guest house, my house too. Make sure nothing is damaged and there are no leaks. I need to pack, and then I'm getting on the road."

"What… *tonight*?"

"Right now," he said, swiveling his seat, stepping down and stalking toward the door. "Sooner I get you back to Potter Lake, the sooner we can be done being friendly."

twenty-six

. . .

TAJ

ONE WEEK LATER

I was ignoring Evonne, for real this time.

Not like all the times I couldn't see her because I was working, or because she was working, or because it was too late to roll by her place and say hi. I was actively ignoring her. Had been since the trip. Which wasn't fair to either of us, but until I could figure out what I was doing, what the near future and far future looked like for me, it was best to step away, to let things drift naturally back to where they had been before we had that tempting, sweet kiss, and almost had sweaty sex on the piano.

Before I seduced her with wine and boozy donuts.

Before I begged her to go with me to my hometown, threw her in with a bunch of people she didn't know, and watched her handle it like a rockstar. Everybody in my life loved her.

Before I fell for her, too. Just enough to not want her to get close to anyone else, including Terrell.

I'd already beat myself up over being jealous. It was a

malicious comment, but what Evonne had said was true. He took my spot, and the group shot to stardom. He'd known Evonne first, had slept with her first, had first followed the supple landscape of her skin, had first experienced her every curve. And didn't even appreciate it.

The drive from Jacksonville that night, all four painful hours of it, was deathly quiet. She didn't ask questions, make observations, ask to listen to her ridiculous podcasts. She threw a jacket over her head, turned away from me, and either slept or pretended to sleep the entire way.

She conveniently awoke as soon as I pulled into the garage, and the overhead light came on, hopped out of the car, popped the trunk, made the Herculean lift of her suitcase from the cavity, and rolled it to the guest house without a word.

I needed to check the place out, but I decided to let it sit. I'd head over there the next day.

The house was fine, of course. The generator did its job until the primary power source had been restored. Everything was working; there were no leaks, nothing out of place except for the game of UNO still sitting out on the coffee table in my bedroom.

"You need to fix this, baby," my mother advised. I called her the day after we'd returned to check-in. And pout. "Somehow, some way."

"Fix what? We were just messing around. Nothin' special."

A chuckle came from deep in her throat. "Boy, if you don't stop."

"What? We were."

"You are well on your way to being in love with that girl. You want it to be casual and some fun, but you can't tell the heart what to do. So she didn't tell you about Terrell? Well, I wouldn't either. I wouldn't want to think about his ass, I wouldn't want to say his name and I definitely wouldn't want to tell my current that I got used, abused and hung out to dry by some big head celebrity."

She gave one last harrumph, and finished with, "I never liked that boy."

She was right, and I knew that and had even told myself the same thing. None of that was why I'd been avoiding her.

Not even the... *feelings* part.

"I don't know what I'm supposed to offer her. Guys Next Door is up in the air right now. I'm getting brochures for master's programs at Healy. I was so stagnant for so long, and now I have way too many options. I honestly do not know what I'm doing. I'm supposed to drag somebody through that with me?"

"That's called life, son. What is she asking for? What is she asking you to offer her?"

"Nothing," I said, tossing the colorful Healy University brochure on the kitchen counter. "She's not asking me for anything. She wants to be independent, find herself, fight for herself."

"A good sign, I think," she replied. "Nothing worse than a girl hanging onto you from your wallet strings. You told her all about your life, your awards, your embarrassment of riches. She wasn't interested in any of that but *you*. And boy, is she into you. I know you two thought you couldn't be heard, but we actually had to put in earplugs the other morning. Sounded like baby-making to me."

"Ma!" I shouted. She cackled loudly. I was hot and a little lightheaded at the thought that my parents could hear us that morning. It was the furthest thought from my mind.

She sighed, simmering down. "Well, son... I hope you get this worked out. I like her for you. And I know you saw those childbearing hips—"

"Ma, come on. I mean damn!"

"Let me go before you hang up on me. But think about

this: I need some grandchildren. And you need some love in your life. Go get that girl."

That was days ago. And I'd love nothing more than to go get that girl, but she never answered the door when I knocked, never replied to my texts, never picked up my calls. I stared in the direction of the guest house, willing her to call me, text me, grab a bottle of that cheap wine she drank, call me *Nurse Dude* and let everything be the way it had been.

But it wouldn't happen. Evonne was stubborn. Crazy, because that's what I liked about her.

I grabbed my keys from the counter, pushed my wallet into my pocket, and headed out to the garage.

———

Evonne had mentioned Thai Bistro a few times, and since I was driving by, I swerved into the parking lot and walked in. I was headed toward the bar when I heard my name.

"Taj! Hey Taj! Back here!"

I turned to see the ladies from the Curl & Dye, Leslie and Tamera, a few people I didn't know and a couple of guys I knew from the barbershop; KC, Erik, who I knew was dating Tamera and Kendrick, the head barber at Guys N' Dolls.

I couldn't very well turn away since they'd recognized me and called me over, so I placed an order for a beer and a shot of whiskey and told the bartender I would be at the rowdy table in the back.

"Hi, Taj," Tamera asked, wedging a chair at the table to make room for me to sit. "My cut is still looking nice, but why don't you stop by Guys N' Dolls this weekend, let me touch it up?"

My drinks showed up, as well as a refill on table snacks. I helped myself to a few fries. "You're cutting at Guys N' Dolls?"

"Yeah, they've taken back over the Dolls side. We'd been

using it as a lounge since we send the ladies over to Leslie's, but we have the room, while her shop is being renovated."

I nodded as KC spoke. I was getting all of the information I needed: Curl & Dye was not closing. Evonne could work in the interim. That eased worries that I didn't know I had.

"Hey, KC… I know you're up on what's available, building wise. If I wanted to buy a spot and build it out— not anything big, but I'm not talking a storefront either. What's the likelihood of finding that out here?"

"You mean a commercial space?"

I gave him a single nod, then brought the bottle of beer to my lips. He folded his arms across his chest and glanced at Leslie, who had lived in Potter Lake her whole life.

"There are a few empty buildings over on the old side," she said. "They're near the train tracks."

"No, no. I'm thinking about a studio. Can't record with a train rolling by every hour." Everyone at the table burst into laughter, and then there were apologies all around when I didn't get the joke.

"The train doesn't run anymore," said Kendrick. "It used to be the main method of delivery back in the day, but now they truck everything on the highway. It'll be quiet. There are a few buildings still standing, but I'd want to knock them down and start from the ground up. They don't meet code."

"Especially since this last storm has taught us how these old buildings don't stand up to modern weather," Leslie said. "It's only going to get worse."

"True that," I agreed. I tossed back my shot of whiskey and grimaced. It was strong. Just what I needed to numb my feelings.

"So, can I be nosy?" Tamera started.

"Tam!" Leslie interrupted.

"What? He's right here!" Ignoring everyone else, Tamera leaned in, resting her chin in her palm. "Evonne told us about that group you were in, Guys Next Door. Does asking about a studio mean you're going back? Or... maybe you'll be recording on your own?"

I shrugged. "To be honest, Tamera, I don't know. I haven't made any real decisions. There's talk. I haven't decided to go one way or the other."

"*Ohhh.* So then you haven't decided about Evonne, either."

"Decided what about Evonne?"

Tamera shrugged, finding her beer to be extremely interesting.

"Seriously," I asked again. "Decided what about Evonne?"

"I guess she's waiting to see if you're going or staying. If you're going back, then you wouldn't want to be with her. Why bring sand to the beach, know what I'm saying? Why would you want her, when you could have any of those girls with their tits out in the front row?"

"Evonne thinks I wouldn't want to date her if I went back to the group?"

There were nods all around the table. Guaranteed they'd discussed me and her and the group ad nauseam at the salon.

"Last she heard you were going back. You haven't talked to her, to clear up that assumption," said Leslie.

"It's not like it's been six months, y'all. I just needed a couple of days to—" The downturn of Leslie's mouth was so pitiful. Disappointment radiated from her face. I gave up, slouching in my seat. "Anyway, she won't answer the phone."

"Because now," said Tamera, "she thinks you're trying to get in the same room with her so you can have a proper breakup discussion. She don't want to hear that shit. And you don't need to say it. If it's over, let it be over."

"I don't want it to be— I'm fucking this up," I said. "I don't know how to make this right again."

"Just talk to her, man," said KC, pointing with the neck of his beer. "Trust me; you won't win her over by playing with her emotions. Be open, be honest with your feelings, if you like her like that."

"If I could get in the door, I would. I can't just bust in there."

"What about something you two like to do? A game or something," Leslie suggested. "Invite her to do that. All you need is something to break the ice."

"She's at home right now, Taj." Tamera picked up a slim device and slid her thumb across the face. "We invited her out, but she wanted to sit at home and listen to some podcasts with her sister. I'll text her that you're coming and ask her to let you in. But promise me you're not trying to get in there so you can dump her. She doesn't need that."

I scooted my chair back and dug my wallet out of my pocket to pay my bar tab.

"I promise. I'm not doing anything like that."

twenty-seven

. . .

EVONNE

"She should have known his ass was waiting downstairs! You always take the gun cause he ain't dead! I swear these bitches be so dumb!"

"Mmhmm! You think you're safe, but his ass will pop right back up."

Ebony's voice was tinny as it came through the phone, bouncing off the tile in the bathroom while I finished my evening routine. We had a standing date of listening to The Butler Did It together whenever we could, and I'd been waiting to listen to the newest episode until Ebony got off work. I broadcasted the playback from my laptop while we sat on the phone together.

I felt the faint rumble of the garage door rolling up. Taj was leaving the house, finally. He'd been trying to get over here or to get me on the phone for days. Probably to tell me that he was going back to the group, thanks for all the sex, but now if I would just be a good little tenant and not bother him and his groupies, as agreed.

I wasn't interested in that conversation.

A few days after I'd returned from Jacksonville, I'd been on the phone with Grandma Bobbie, filling her in on my weekend. I left out most of it;… her eighty-eight-year-old ears didn't need all of that. Before we hung up, she told me to hold on. Somebody wanted to talk to me.

"Evonne? So you're back from Florida, then?"

I sighed. I was not in the mood for another round. "Yes, Mama. I'm back."

"Well… all right. Glad you made it."

I thought she'd hand the phone back to Grandma Bobbie, but she continued. "I uh… well, I was at the mall with the boys, and I went by the Williams Sonoma store. You know I don't need a single thing for the kitchen, but I like to look. And I saw some emerald green Le Creuset plates. You know the big, thick square ones? Anyway, I picked up a set. I… I don't suppose we'll be seeing you soon, but I'll send them with Ebony the next time she's headed that way."

I stood in the middle of the salon with a hand on one hip and the phone to my ear, blinking back tears. I needed to be still mad at her. But I took it— the gesture and the phone call — for what it was meant to be—an apology.

And did what I always did. Let it go.

"Thought it would be nice to spruce up your place with your favorite color," she said.

"Thank you, Mama. I appreciate it. I do." Then I apologized that I had to hang up because I was at the salon, slid the phone away, and wiped my cheeks dry.

It wouldn't be the last time she let her mouth run away with her. And I realized where I'd gotten the same habit.

I shouldn't have said what I said to Taj. I regretted it the minute it flew from my mouth and had regretted it every moment since. It was cruel and mean and taunting. I was so afraid of becoming like my mother, saying things to make people angry, to elicit any kind of response, even if it was negative.

I did not want to be that woman, but I had been her with him.

Taj didn't deserve that kind of woman.

That wasn't why I hadn't been answering his calls or opening the door when he came by, though. I didn't want him to make up with me because it was the easiest thing to do, because we lived so close to one another.

I wanted him to make up with me because he felt something for me. If I was some friendly fun, then we could go back to being landlord and tenant, and everything would be fine.

As soon as I got over him.

I patted my skin dry and smeared moisturizing cream over my face before picking up the laptop and the phone and carting them both to the bedroom. I set the computer on the side table and set the phone on its charging mat, then reached for the light summer blanket that covered the queen size bed. I'd prefer a bed like Taj's, with the high padded headboard in a dark wood, but beggars couldn't be choosers.

I'd already decided that I would get an apartment downtown when my lease was up. All that talk about being mature and adult, if things didn't work out, was some bullshit. I didn't want to be living here when the parade of women came traipsing through for *TDub*.

I saw a text roll in from Tamera. She'd been "checking on me" several times a day since I'd given them the rundown of my short-lived relationship with my landlord. "That's why I told your nosey asses that I wasn't planning to make a move on him," I'd told her while packing up my station at the salon. We would be working out of Guys N' Dolls while KC and his dad were having Curl & Dye renovated. *Better than ever*, is what Leslie had said, her excitement about the salon bolstered.

"This was more fun when we were giggling and daydreaming and now…" Dejected, I moved around the piles of dirt and debris, tossing things into crates for the guys to move them over.

Tamera shrugged and offered condolences. But she also said he would be back. "They always come back, Evonne. Give him time and let it happen."

"I won't hold my breath," I'd told her.

The podcast steadily ramped to the climax of the case, when the killer was captured, then they broke down the trial and verdict. It was the best moment of every episode, one we always anticipated, so I ignored Tamera's clingy check-in and made a note to call her when the broadcast was over.

I slid under the covers, my ears tuned so carefully to the episode that the sound of pounding at my front door genuinely made me jump. I pressed pause on the computer and whispered to Ebony, "Did you hear that?"

"Hear what?"

"It was—"

It was a heavy thud, the edge of a fist against the steel door. The sound was terrifying.

"That!"

"That's somebody at your door, Vonnie. Maybe Taj is coming back. You should open the door this time."

"Nuh uh, I heard Taj leave an hour ago. Who's at my door?"

"Girl, I don't know! Go see!"

I huffed and grabbed the phone, then rolled out of bed, threw on a robe, and headed out to the hallway. "Be ready to hang up and dial 911 if I scream."

"Vonne, you're so overdramatic. A killer wouldn't knock on your door," said Ebony. I swear I could always hear when she was rolling her eyes.

I moved through the kitchen, grabbing a knife from the butcher block as I passed it. "Killers knock all the time, Eb.

They want you to think they're nice and normal, just neighborly. Then you open the door, and they pounce."

"Well, check the peephole thing."

I stopped in front of the door, in the darkened hallway, and tried to look through the peephole, but I didn't see anything.

"Nobody's out there!" I whispered into the phone.

"Evonne?" Called a male voice. "I know you're home. Can we talk?"

Oh, fuck. I heaved a long, loud lungful of air and snatched the door open. I stood in the entryway in a robe thrown over a bralette and boy shorts, phone in one hand, butcher knife in the other.

"What the fuck are you doing?"

Taj jumped back almost a foot, nearly dropping the box in his hands. "Shit!" he screeched. "It's me, Evonne!"

"I didn't hear you come back home. Your ass almost got so fucking murdered, Nurse Dude."

"Well, good! Then I'd be on one of those podcasts, and you'd pay attention to me. Could you put the knife down?"

Taj's eyes were huge; he crouched a foot from me like I would actually stab him.

I exhaled another breath and turned around, tossing the knife and the phone onto the kitchen counter.

"So... can I come in?"

"I mean, the place is yours. Probably can't stop you."

He did so, closing the door behind him. "You scare me. Seriously, you scare the shit out of me, Evonne."

"You were the one beating down my door," I reminded him.

"Tamera was supposed to tell you I was coming."

I flipped on a few lights and continued into the kitchen. Since I was up, I may as well have a nerve settling glass of wine. "Where did you see Tamera? Do you want some wine? It's not Grand Reserve or whatever fancy shit you drink."

"Sure," he said, joining me in the kitchen. "I saw her at Thai Bistro. Like… everybody was there."

"Oh yeah," I muttered. I grabbed a couple of stemless wine glasses from the cabinet and poured us both a few swallows. I handed Taj's to him and leaned against the counter. "It's Cake Night."

"Cake night?"

"Group date night." I rolled my eyes. "I always have to close so Leslie and Tamera can go sit up under their men at Thai Bistro or the bowling alley or the movie theater. You know…*caking*. Flirting, mooning over each other, like they're still dating or whatever."

"Oh. Caking." He took a larger than normal gulp of wine. Understandably, he had nerves to settle too. "I've learned a new term, I guess."

"That'll be useful for you when you start bringing your women through."

"Evonne, we said we wouldn't do this. We wouldn't be immature and childish, right?"

"Yeah, well…" I slurped a loud mouth full of wine. Then sighed. "I'm not as big of a person as I was a week ago. My nasty attitude isn't gonna stop you from fucking everything on two legs, the way famous people do, so…."

"Evonne, can we pull back for—"

"Why do you have that?" I eyed the UNO box that he had brought in.

He held it up like I couldn't see the logo on it. "It's why I came down. Well, it's not why I came down. It was a flimsy excuse to get in the door."

"You don't need a flimsy excuse to get in the door. You own the house, Taj."

"I thought since we didn't get to finish our game of UNO that night…"

"Whose fault was that?"

Taj's brows shot up. "*Somebody* started talking about sweaty piano sex, so it definitely wasn't me, Evonne."

"So… what? Do you want to finish our game? Just randomly came down here after a week of not talking to me, to play a stupid card game?"

"UNO is not a stupid card game." He opened the box and pulled out the giant stack of cards, then fanned them out. "I want to play one last game. For your heart."

I blinked. "For my heart."

"Yeah. If I win, I get your heart."

"What in the Love & Basketball, cornball ass, *I saw this in a movie—*"

A muffled snicker came from the phone on the counter. I'd forgotten that I was talking to Ebony and never hung up. Now she was giggling on speakerphone and eavesdropping our conversation.

"I'm sorry, but that's cute as fuck, Vonnie. Stop acting silly, girl. If you don't take him back, I will."

"Goodnight, Eb," I called before I pressed the button to end the call. I shrugged. "She was supposed to call 911 if you were a serial killer."

"Not a serial killer."

"Taj—"

"Evonne, I'm asking you to point to a place where we can play this game. We can talk while we play. I'm serious."

I groaned, but pushed off of the cabinet and waved him to my bedroom.

Inside, my heart was doing flip-flops all up and through my chest.

———

"Draw four, sucka."

I'd come out of the gate, both guns blazing with no intention of losing. I played every Draw Two, Draw Four, and Wild card I picked up and made him draw and draw and draw until his hands were full of cards.

"You know, it doesn't seem like you want me to win your heart."

He reached for the stack of cards in the middle of the bed, where we'd decided to play, then added four cards to his ridiculous hand.

"You want me to throw the game to prove I want you to have my heart? I'm playing to win."

"And what happens if you win?"

"Then I win, Nurse Dude."

"Mercy, if I admit something to you?"

"What?"

"Okay. I miss you."

My heart lurched. "Of course you do. I'm a goddamn delight."

"That you are," he agreed. "I wasn't talking about physically, though. You bring a certain quality to my life that I didn't realize I'd been missing. And a lot of noise. And a sudden awareness of the information overload that is a podcast. I caught myself listening to This Fly House yesterday."

I giggled. "Taj. You didn't."

"Did so! I listened to a couple of episodes, one on defrosting your freezer and one on winterizing your home. Useful information."

I noted, behind the hands full of cards, the smirk on his lips.

"You're silly," I murmured. I was touched and beginning to soften towards him. I laid down a card I knew he had plenty of, in color. He seemed relieved to be getting rid of cards. "But that is cute."

"Also..."

He cleared his throat, which tipped me off that this admission was going to be much more serious than the previous one had been. "You...were right. About what you said about Terrell. I never really dealt with losing my spot to him. I just...I saw him taking another thing that was supposed to be mine—"

"Yours?" I butted in, seriously asking the question. Because last I had heard, we were having some fun.

"Mine, Evonne," he repeated. "You know what I mean when I say mine. I'm the only one that feels more than he expected to? I'm the only jealous fool out here?"

I shook my head, refusing to give voice to what he already knew. I was seething with jealousy over what he could have if he chose to go back to Guys Next Door... pussy galore. I couldn't and didn't want to compete.

He pushed out a breath from the depth of his lungs and rearranged the cards in his hand. "None of that was about you... not directly. But I do wish I had known that it was Terrell earlier because I would have driven to Atlanta myself to knock him on his ass."

"Taj, I'm so sorry..."

I laid my cards down and buried my face in my hands so he couldn't see the shame. "I should have been wide open about him when you told me about Guys Next Door. I knew it, and I fought with myself about it, and I took the coward's way out because I figured I would never have to tell you about him, either because he was never coming back to the group or because you and I wouldn't work out and—"

Taj threw down his cards and crawled over the game toward me. He yanked my hands down and covered my mouth with his.

I cupped his face and held him close to me as we kissed hungrily— passionate moaning, lip biting, tongue sucking until we had to pull apart because we were both out of breath.

"I have definitely missed that," said Taj.

I heaved the longest, loudest breath of relief. "God, me too." Taj was paying more attention to my breasts, nearly popping out of the lace bralette I was going to wear to bed. "Titties, huh?"

He laughed, then flipped to sit next to me, up against the pillows. He was comfy casual in sweatpants, a t-shirt and white athletic socks.

"So…after everything went down with Terrell, I told the guys I needed to think a little longer. I have some ideas, and if I can get them to agree, it'll make it easier to go back. But I don't want going back to the group to mean I can't build a life and live it. I worked too hard to beat cancer, to be a nurse…"

He laid a hand on top of mine and gave me a squeeze. "But baby, even if I do go back…on the stage, off the stage, Taj or TDub, I'm the same dude."

"You say that now, but—"

"Evonne," he interrupted, squeezing me again. "I know what it is to lose something that means something to you. I would never risk losing you. What I do for a living makes no difference in what I feel for you. Or what I want with you. I mean, if you want it, too."

"Depends on what you want. This *friendly* shit isn't going to cut it for me because if you're mine, I want you to be mine… and I feel like if we're just fucking, I don't mean anything to you, like my opinion on what you do with your life doesn't matter, but I do really want something real, and I want to be your biggest supporter, but if you go back to Guys Next Door, I can't fight every groupie bitch that thinks she knows you because she memorized your Wikipedia page—"

"Oh my God, Evonne…" He pinched the bridge of his nose and tried not to laugh at me. It wasn't working. "Is this what happens when we go a week without seeing each other? Your words get all stored up, and you have to let them out all at once?"

I rolled my eyes, but I had to laugh at myself. I did want to get all the words out before he came down here to give me his goodbye speech. I told Tamera that I didn't want to hear that from him. We could let this fade away.

He leaned over so he could reach for something in his pocket and pulled out his phone. "I know you don't get into Guys Next Door, but I wrote something a long time ago that I think fits this situation perfectly. Can I play it for you?"

"You always want me to listen to your lil' friends," I grumbled, but gestured toward the phone. "Play it, I guess."

"It's called *Stay*." He pressed the play button and scooted back, dropped an arm over my shoulders and drew me closer to him.

The track began with a deep voice that I now knew was Cash, inviting someone, presumably a girl, to sit back and listen. The rest of the guys rolled in after him in perfect, beautiful harmony, apologizing for leaving a girl crying and all alone but that tonight he wanted to start all over again, to put trust on the line, to be more than friends.

He was asking her to stay.

Taj leaned into me and, very quietly, began to sing, falling in with the bridge.

"Let's forget yesterday, 'cause I want it bad, let's make love like we never had, the night is almost over, so just stay, stay with me…"

"Aww," I swooned. "I've never heard you sing before, Taj. You have a great voice!"

He dipped his head in what I knew was pure shyness. "I try not to use it to get women. I'm not smooth, but… that's cheap."

"You know how I met Terrell?" I burst into laughter. "He sang to me." Then I sighed. "I *am* a bird."

"You are not a bird. Or a chickenhead or a whore or whatever names he called you to your face or behind your back. You are Evonne *No Middle Name Having Ass* Girard. You are talented and creative, and funny. And so soft but so hard and so sexy and so smart. And… I think I could love you if you let me."

I sat up, then moved to straddle him, settling on his lap. I looped my arms around his neck and kissed him. His hands found their way to my backside.

"You... *think*... you could—"

"Come on, Evonne. I brought the game down here, tried to be romantic about it, but you kicked my ass. I *sang* to you, and I do not sing to women. What do you want from me?"

I was going to joke some more. Lighten the mood some more. Take some more pressure off, but he deserved a serious answer.

"I want to trust you with every part of my life, especially the ugly shit. And I want you to trust me with yours. I want you to call me *Miss Girard* when I get on your nerves. I want you to pick on me about all my podcasts. I want you to mutter under your breath when I set something down on your nice clean counter. I want you to let me ride that mustang, baby."

Taj let out a gut level guffaw. I laughed, too because... shit, that was funny.

"But mostly," I finished, softly, quietly. Vulnerability wasn't my strong suit. It had never benefitted me to put my heart on the line before. "I mostly want *Taj Wright* to want me. *Only* me, no matter what happens with Guys Next Door."

"I do, Evonne. I want you, only you, no matter what happens."

My mouth met his in a crush of lips and the swirl of tongues. He pulled me closer, tightened his arms around me and brought me closer still.

"Baby," he whispered in-between nibbles of my earlobe and soft kisses along my shoulder. "I want to lay here with you and hold you and listen to you ramble about whatever podcast you're obsessed with today. I need to do that every day. Starting today. I mean, rent is still due on the first..."

I giggled. Then dropped a kiss on those thick, suckable

lips. Then I moved back so we could clear the game from the bed.

We were destined to never finish a game of UNO.

"Know what else I want, Taj?" I stretched out next to his long, muscular form. He had quickly removed his sweatpants and t-shirt and crawled into my bed in his normal sleep attire of absolutely nothing.

"What else do you want, Evonne?" He pulled me to him, closing his arms around me. I had only slept in his arms for a few nights, but that week away from him had been torture. I relaxed, sinking into my usual places against him, feeling like I was home again.

"I want boozy donuts and fancy wine. But also cheap wine. And luxury condoms."

He laughed. Hard. "You're a lot of fun, Evonne."

I tilted my chin up. "But?"

"But nothing." He bent to kiss me, then kiss me again, then rolled us over, so he was on top, settling into his usual spot between my thighs. "You're... a lot of fun."

I was already making short work of my bralette and boy shorts. I'd left them on while we played because if Taj was breaking up with me, I wanted him to see what he was giving up.

And because if he *wasn't* breaking up with me, I didn't want to have to work for it.

I accepted the warm, heavy weight of him on top of me, his body meshing with mine. We kissed and kissed and kissed like we hadn't seen each other in weeks instead of seven entire days. The sensation of Taj growing harder, pressed into my belly between us made me heady.

"Condom," I gasped when he let me come up for air. I felt his body freeze, saw his eyes slide closed.

"*Fuck*. I forgot." He started to sit up, then search one side of the bed and then the other. "I'm going to run upstairs for a quick minute—"

"Whoa, wait. Check the bottom drawer of the nightstand."

He moved over and reached down enough to open the drawer. And laughed.

I sat up, amused with myself as he brought the brand new box of NAKED condoms to the bed. "Open them," I told him. "So you know you can trust me. No holes in the condoms or tricky shit like that."

"You think you are so funny." He ripped the cellophane off the package, opened the box and pulled out a few small packets, then put the box back in the drawer.

"I am so funny. Want me to put it on?"

"No," he said. "You take too long, trying to be sexy with it. Drives me crazy."

I laughed, watching him roll it on entirely faster and less artistically than I would. He got back into the bed and came to me again, this time fully sheathed.

"I can't lie, Taj. I have missed you these last few days."

"I missed you, too," he said, his lips a feather-soft whisper against mine. "I'm sorry I stayed away. I had to get my head on straight."

"So… it's straight now?"

"Depends." He paused for a beat, then asked. "Do I have you back, Miss Girard?"

I grinned. "As fuck, Nurse Dude."

My head rocked back, and my eyes slid closed as his girth pushed into me. Taj clasped his hands in mine and used our jumbled fingers as leverage to use every bit of his strength to bring pleasured moans and grunts, skin slapping against skin, bodies grinding together, trying desperately to be one being.

"Vonne—"

He shuddered, choking on the word like it was stuck in his throat, and that was the little bit that could eke out, otherwise, he was going to scream.

I felt the same.

"Yes! Oh my... *fuck*! Go!"

I ground my body into his, hoping to bring him with me as I fell over the cliff. I felt him pulse, and I knew he was there with me. I held onto him, my nails digging into his shoulders through the final throes.

When we finished, his body came to rest on top of mine. I closed my arms around him and listened to his breathing go from deep, air sucking pants to steady breaths; until the sweat dried on our skin, and our body temperatures returned to normal.

Only then did he roll to the side, then flip onto his back.

"Vonne."

"Mmmmm?" I scooted up close to him and tossed a leg over his. He brought an arm around me.

"Next time we go to Jacksonville, we gotta stay in the basement."

"We do? Why?"

A laugh rumbled through his chest. "Because my mom said she heard us, that morning."

"*Ohhh.*" I giggled, feeling like I should be more embarrassed, but was actually quite proud that Theresa had brought it up. We'd had a *good* time. "See, I told you about disrespecting your parents in their house."

"My mom wants grand babies, so she doesn't have a problem with us having sex. She wants us to make the grand babies where she can't hear us."

"I'm just happy that I get an invite back, Taj."

He kissed my forehead and yawned. "They'd almost rather see you than me. My brothers made sure to tell me that they like you a lot. And so do the guys, even though you don't—"

"Stop it! I like them fine; I just didn't want to see Terrell's ass."

"That's why you never heard any of their songs."

I nodded. "So, he's officially gone?"

"Officially gone, whether I come back or not."

"That's good. I suppose I can listen to your lil group's next album then."

He sat up a little to stretch and turn off the bedside lamp, then relaxed again.

"You heard what I said, right, Evonne? About how I could see myself in love with you?"

I recognized this for what it was. He wanted me to say it.

"I heard you. I could see myself in love with you too, Nurse Dude."

epilogue

. . .

Taj

ONE YEAR *Later*

"Don't forget, Mrs. Vaughn; I won't be here for a few weeks. Don't be afraid to call Doc Moore's patient line. There's always a nurse on duty to answer questions, and then you don't have to walk down here. Okay?"

She nodded and smiled. She had lipstick on her teeth.

Mrs. Vaughn always nodded and smiled but would still come down to the clinic even when I wasn't on shift. I'd rallied behind her though, finally persuading the staff to stop treating her like a crazy old lady. She trusted us.

I put my foot down with Officer Vaughn about leaving her alone, too. He finally put in for a shift change, and this was the last week that she'd be by herself at night. During the day, she would be at Primrose Gardens, the Assisted Living Center. He'd pick her up from there and bring her home, which made me feel better about signing out for the day and not returning for a few weeks.

I turned over my patients at shift change, clocked out, and picked up my nylon backpack, slinging it over my shoulder. "Okay, y'all... I'm out of here."

"Bye, Taj!" The team of night nurses beamed bright smiles and waved. "Good luck on tour! We're all going to the Atlanta show, so shout us out!"

I was still shy about the whole town knowing I was *TDub* from The Guys Next Door. Potter Lake was so small, though, that it hardly made a difference. I was still Taj Wright, RN.

And I would always be Nurse Dude.

"I sure will."

It had been a few months since the announcement that I had rejoined The Guys Next Door and that we were working on a new album and a mini-tour. Potter Lake Times had come out to the house to do a big spread on their "celebrity" resident. I had the chance to tell my story, cancer fight, and all.

KC said it was nice to not be the celebrity, for once, and officially welcomed me to the Potter Lake community.

I built out a small space for Guys Next Door to use in Potter Lake, which made it easier for me to keep up my hours while we wrote, rehearsed and recorded. I didn't need the money, but I needed to work, and my patients needed me. I wanted to keep serving the Mrs. Vaughn's and Ms. Doris' of the world.

After the tour, Guys Next Door would go on another hiatus. Cash wanted to spend more time with his kids, Quise would have two of his brothers in college by then, and Dav needed time to plan a wedding.

And I would be starting work on my MSN and Oncology Nurse Practitioner Certification. Ms. Doris planned to mentor me and was riding me hard about it. I was honored that she had offered.

It didn't take long for me to move Evonne into the house with me. It seemed silly to keep switching from my place to hers when our places were one hundred fifty feet apart. A surprise to no one, Ebony promptly moved into the guest house.

A surprise to everyone was Evonne offering to host the Girard's for dinner. The entire evening was pleasant. Rhonda and Evonne were making tenuous steps... there was a lot of work and healing ahead, but both were making an effort.

I still needed to pack for the twenty city, southeastern tour, but first, I drove across the bridge to the Curl & Dye, which had finally reopened after the post-storm renovation. The new salon was sunny and bright due to more windows, and much bigger, with upgraded technology. Leslie didn't want to change too much about the shop though, so it still had that hometown feel that the regulars loved.

"Hey, Taj!"

Tamera stood at the front door with both hands full, but she offered a cheek. I brushed my lips against her skin. I dipped to Evonne's chair to interrupt an intricate style she was managing to pull off using two curling rods with a kiss to her cheek as well.

"You got an opening?" I asked Tamera, rubbing my palm over the longer than usual length atop my head. "I need one good cut before I hit the road."

"Go ahead and have a seat in my chair," she said, stocking a few containers back in the cabinet upfront. "Although, why you don't let your fiancée cut your hair, I don't know."

"Because she scares the shit out of me," I quipped, sinking into the chair I knew well by now. Evonne glared, then snapped her curling rods in my direction. "See? No telling what she could do if she got mad at me. I can't hit the stage looking like my woman was mad at me."

"I would never do that to you, Nurse Dude."

"You *would* try something you heard about on a podcast. No, thanks."

I picked up a magazine and flipped through it. Tamera finally grabbed a cape and fluttered it out, letting it settle around me before tightening the Velcro straps around my neck.

"So, Taj... Evonne..." Ms. Cara came out from under the dryer, clutching a magazine she'd been pretending to read to her chest. I swore that woman stayed in the beauty shop to be in the middle of gossip. "Are there any wedding plans to share?"

"We just got engaged last week, Ms. Cara," Evonne said. "We're not making any plans until Taj is back from tour and he starts his degree program. He's got enough on his plate, and I'm not in a hurry to get married."

"Although," I added, "my mother is in marathon runner starter position, waiting for us to pull the trigger. I want to see how long it takes to drive her crazy before I tell her she can start planning."

"You'll be getting married in Jacksonville?" Tamera asked, before flipping her clippers on.

"Yep. Evonne wants a beach wedding."

She beamed at me. I winked back.

"That'll be beautiful. Of course, it'll be perfect because it's the two of you," swooned Ms. Cara. "We got married in Las Vegas. Garth and I did it up. I had the whole package, in one of those cathedrals, the long fairytale dress, and everything. You'd never know from the pictures that we were in Vegas. And then after the ceremony, we gambled and partied all night with our family and friends. That's what it's all about, you know. Not an expensive show, just loving on your loved ones."

"We agree," said Evonne. "It'll be a big party. With rings and vows."

"If I may continue to be nosy, I hope there are plans to start a family."

Tamera laughed. "Ms. Cara, can they *breathe*?"

"Well, when it's time, dear."

"We might get a dog," I answered. Ms. Cara frowned. I

laughed. "Chemotherapy and radiation can destroy sperm cells, so we're not sure if we can." I caught Evonne's eye. "We're having fun practicing, though. Getting real good at it."

Ms. Cara blushed. That's what she got for asking.

"You're good to go, Taj." Tamera hung up her clippers and brushed errant hairs from my neck and shoulders. "Check out upfront."

I pulled the cape off and dropped it into my chair, then moved to the front counter so Tamera could ring me up. I tucked away the receipt and waved to Evonne, but she held up a finger for me to wait.

So I did, watching her put her irons on their stands and slip off her apron. She whispered something to her customer, who nodded, then rushed to the front of the shop.

"Outside," she whispered, then tugged me by the arm out of the front door. We walked to my car, where Evonne stopped and turned to face me. The emerald that I'd slipped on her finger the week before glistened in the sunlight as she nervously turned it around on her finger.

"What's up, Vonne? Why'd we have to come outside?"

"Because I need to tell you something. I wanted to wait and tell you tonight. You know, do it special. But hearing you talk about a family, I can't wait another second."

My heart dropped to the pit of my stomach. She must have received the results back from the sperm analysis I'd asked my doctor to run. I needed to know, before I promised Evonne the moon and the stars if I could even give her children.

"Tell me. Is something wrong?"

"No." She shook her head. "Something is right. *Everything* is right, I mean... *Baby* Wright, right." She gazed up at me, those big almond shaped, beautiful brown eyes glistening with unshed tears.

I held my breath for a few moments because I wasn't sure I'd heard what I heard. *Baby?*

"Baby Wright... as in *our* baby? Are you serious? Don't play with me, Evonne."

"I am as serious as a positive pregnancy test!" She began to laugh, and I wanted to laugh along, but I wasn't all the way there yet.

When we got very serious, very quickly, and started talking about getting married, we decided to face potential infertility head on and together, the same way we had done everything, including me rejoining the group and going back to school.

Waiting for the results of the sperm analysis was paralyzing. I almost didn't propose to Evonne, afraid that if I couldn't give her babies, she might not want to marry me. She quickly convinced me, when she saw the emerald and platinum ring, that I was ridiculous.

No matter what happens is what we had agreed.

"You... we... so...when..."

"Taj..." Evonne smirked, tilting her head to the side. "You know *exactly* when."

I did. I smiled at myself, recalling it. We'd been diligent about protection, even if I could be shooting blanks because we wanted to be *sure*, sure that we wanted children. Whatever happened, happened, but we didn't want to be careless about it.

Unless we were both fresh out of the shower, on our mutual day off and feeling particularly lusty since we'd had the *ain't no way you're getting rid of me and you're gonna have to marry my ass* conversation.

YOLO.

I shook my head, my mind a dizzying blur. My swimmers worked! And I was going to be a dad!

"Okay. So. Does anyone else know?"

"Ebony, because I made her go with me to buy the test. And my doctor, who confirmed the blood test this morning—"

"This…Evonne! Why didn't you—"

"Because I didn't want to get your hopes up! But I got sick, and I *never* get sick, and I had a feeling. I wanted to give you some good news. There's no worry about your sperm count, baby. We are definitely very pregnant."

It finally sunk in. My brain exploded, and so did my heart. I was crazy in love with this woman, and we were going to have a baby. I grabbed her, clutching her to me. I could not hug her tightly enough.

But then I let go, because I was worried about holding her too tight.

And then I came crashing down at the thought of leaving her. *Them.*

"But I shouldn't be gone—"

"Don't even think about it. You have to do what you were born to do. And then come back to me. To *us.* And start on your degree. And get one of those rooms in the ivory tower ready for your *baby.*"

She sucked her teeth, rolled her eyes, and finished, "And, I don't know, write some songs for your lil' group and their next album."

"I… okay. I… I don't know what to say—"

"I didn't think it would happen this quickly. I mean, we just got engaged, and I know it's so fast, but please just say you're happy."

"Evonne, I am so happy." I cupped her face and brought her lips to mine in a long, sweet kiss. "Mother of my baby."

"Our baby," she reminded me.

"*Our* baby," I repeated. And kissed her again and again until she pulled back.

"Okay, okay… I have to go finish my client's hair, so we'll talk more tonight. We have so much to do—I want to start writing episodes on safe products to use while you're pregnant and how to style through pregnancy. Oh!And I need to research stuff like postpartum hair loss. There's a podcast I was listening to—"

"Evonne…" I cocked my head back and laughed into the warm spring air. "Go. We'll talk tonight. And tell them, all of them, Ms. Cara and especially Tamera. I need her to watch you like a hawk."

"I would be happy to share our news." Evonne was beaming. Glowing. Beautiful. "I love you, Nurse Dude."

"I love you too, Miss Girard. Soon to be Mrs. Wright."

I watched through the brand new double pane windows as she went back inside the salon, happily bounded back to her chair, and looped the apron back over her head.

I watched her, with a smile that went from ear to ear, say something to Tamera.

Then I watched Tamera stand stock still and cover her mouth with both hands. Evonne nodded. Tamera glanced out the door to me and then back to Evonne. Ms. Cara got up and wrapped her up in a hug, then joined by Tamera.

Evonne was radiant, delirious with happiness.

Making her happy was something I was going to get to do for as long as possible.

———

Want to be the first to know what happens next in Potter Lake? Join the newsletter— and get a free short story!

Read the next book in the series- Home for the Holidays

acknowledgments

I struggle with this part because I know I'll miss someone! If I don't call you out, you know the old saying… charge it to my head and not my heart!

Always got to thank the fam first. They are my staunchest supporters who love me in spite of.

Thanks as well to the #friendfam, who are always there to offer an idea and endless support, who answer dumb questions and give me brilliant ideas. Most especially, my author frands, my sister friends, my brunch divas, and my improperly coiffured trollops. You *all* saved this book.

I also need to thank BET for having the *New Edition Movie* available to watch over and over and over. Also, Spotify for having Jodeci *Stay* available to play on repeat for hours. Last but not least, the greatest boy band to ever do it, *NSYNC. Long live Justin, Chris, Joey, Lance & JC— may my fangirl heart never cease to sparkle.

I would be remiss in not thanking those who have shared their stories of survival from the treatment of cancers like Non-Hodgkin Lymphoma. I knew that I was going to write a survivor and the aftermath of living through such a trauma. Your brave and gripping stories gave Taj a full background and a reason to go on.

To the Betas, the proofreaders the '*does this sound dumb*' sounding boards, the cheering section… thank you. You make creating this jumble of words look easy, and I really can't thank you enough.

about the author

Atlanta based women's fiction and romance author DL White began seriously pursuing a writing career in 2011. She harbors a love for coffee and brunch, especially on a patio, but her real obsession is water— lakes, rivers, oceans, waterfalls! On the weekend, you'll probably find her near water and if she's lucky, on an ocean beach.

When not writing books, she devours them. She blogs reviews and thoughts on writing and books at BooksbyDL-White.com. Grab a book by DL White and #*Putitinyourface*.

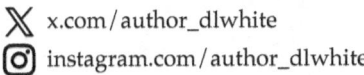

𝕏 x.com/author_dlwhite

instagram.com/author_dlwhite

books by dl white

Find Books and Merch at Booksbydlwhite.com/shop

Brunch at Ruby's, a Ruby's novel

Dinner at Sam's, a Ruby's novel

Beach Thing, a Black Diamond Romance

Elysium, a Black Diamond Vacation Romance

The Pearl at Black Diamond, a Black Diamond Romance

Leslie's Curl & Dye, a Potter Lake Small Town Romance

Second Time Around, a Potter Lake Holiday Short

The Guy Next Door, a Potter Lake Small Town Romance

Home for the Holidays, A Potter Lake Holiday Novella

The Kwanzaa Brunch, a Holiday Short

A Thin Line

The Never List

Hey, Lover, a Second Chance Romance

Unexpected, a holiday short

The Festival at Evergreen Falls

Grumpy Valentine

Calculated Risk *(Coming Spring 2025)*